## *"I want you to think, and think hard," Boyd said.*

"Who's shown an interest in you?" There was an edge to his voice that had her holding back the snide comment she wanted to make. "Someone who calls the station more frequently than usual, who asks to meet you, asks personal questions. Someone who's approached you, asked you out, made a play."

Cilla gave a short, humorless laugh. "You have."

"Remind me to run a make on myself." His voice was deceptively mild, but she caught the underlying annoyance and frustration. "Who else, Cilla?"

"There's no one, no one that's pushed. I get calls—that's the idea. I get some that ask me for a date, some that even send presents. You know, candy-and-flowers types. Nothing very sinister about a bunch of roses."

"There's a lot sinister about death threats."

"Look, this is getting us nowhere, and I'm..." Cilla's words trailed off, and her hand crept slowly toward her throat.

Boyd stiffened. "What is it?"

"There's a man across the street. He's watching the house."

Dear Reader,

Happy New Year and welcome to another exciting month of romance from Silhouette Intimate Moments. We've got another irresistible lineup of books for you, as well as a future treat that I'll be mentioning in a moment. First, though, how about a new book from one of your favorite authors, Nora Roberts? *Night Shift* will enthrall you—and leave you eager to read *Night Shadow*, coming in March. Readers of historical romance may recognize the name Catherine Palmer. Whether you know her name or not, you will undoubtedly enjoy her debut for Silhouette Intimate Moments, *Land of Enchantment*. Round out the month with new books from Sibylle Garrett and Joyce McGill, two more of the authors who make this line so special.

Now for that future treat I mentioned. Next month we're presenting "February Frolics," an entire month made up of nothing but first novels written by authors whose futures look very bright indeed. Here at Silhouette Intimate Moments we're always trying to find fresh new voices in the romance field, and we think we've come up with four of the best. Next month you'll get a chance to see whether you agree with us—and I hope you do!

In coming months, look for new books from more of your favorites: Dallas Schulze, Heather Graham Pozzessere and Marilyn Pappano, to name just a few. And every month, enjoy some of the best books in romance today: Silhouette Intimate Moments.

Leslie J. Wainger
Senior Editor and Editorial Coordinator

# NORA ROBERTS

# Night Shift

SILHOUETTE·INTIMATE·MOMENTS®

Published by Silhouette Books New York

**America's Publisher of Contemporary Romance**

SILHOUETTE BOOKS
300 East 42nd St., New York, N.Y. 10017

NIGHT SHIFT

ISBN: 0-373-07365-8

First Silhouette Books printing January 1991

Printed in the U.S.A.

# NORA ROBERTS

lives in western Maryland with her husband and two children. Nora's book *Irish Thoroughbred*, a Silhouette Romance, was published in 1981 to universal acclaim. Mid-1988 marked the publication of her *fiftieth* Silhouette and the beginning of a new series. A charter member of the Romance Writers of America, Nora Roberts is the first author to win six Golden Medallions, and she entered the RWA Hall of Fame in 1986.

One of Silhouette's most popular and prolific authors, Nora has appeared on CNN and *Good Morning, America*, as well as in articles in the *Washington Post*, the *Baltimore Sun*, the *New York Times* and the *Wall Street Journal*.

---

# AWARDS:

**Romance Writers of America,**
**First Place/Golden Medallion:**
*The Heart's Victory*, Silhouette Special Edition. 1983. Best category sensuous romance.
*Untamed*, Silhouette Romance. 1984. Best traditional romance.
*This Magic Moment*, Silhouette Intimate Moments. 1984. Best contemporary romance.
*Opposites Attract*, Silhouette Special Edition. 1985. Best contemporary romance under 70,000 words.
*A Matter of Choice*, Silhouette Intimate Moments. 1985. Best contemporary romance over 70,000 words.
*One Summer*, Silhouette Special Edition. 1987. Best long contemporary book.
**Georgia Romance Writers of America "Maggie":**
*Partners*, Silhouette Intimate Moments. 1985. Best category contemporary romance.
**Romantic Times "Artie":**
1984 Best category contemporary author.
**Romantic Times "Best Continuing Series":**
1986 The MacGregor Series.
**Romantic Times Reviewers' Choice Awards**
*Reflections*, Silhouette Special Edition. 1984.
*Partners*, Silhouette Intimate Moments. 1985.
*One Summer*, Silhouette Special Edition. 1986.

To Kay in Denver

And with appreciation to the staff of
WQCM

# Chapter 1

"All right, night owls, it's coming up on midnight, and you're listening to KHIP. Get ready for five hits in a row. This is Cilla O'Roarke, and darling, I'm sending this one straight out to you."

Her voice was like hot whiskey, smooth and potent. Rich, throaty, touched with the barest whisper of the South, it might have been fashioned for the airwaves. Any man in Denver who was tuned in to her frequency would believe she was speaking only to him.

Cilla eased up on the pot on the mixer, sending the first of the five promised hits out to her listeners. Music slid into the booth. She could have pulled off her headphones and given herself three minutes and twenty-two seconds of silence. She preferred the sound. Her affection for music was only one of the reasons for her success in radio.

Her voice was a natural attribute. She'd talked herself into her first job—at a low-frequency, low-budget station in rural Georgia—with no experience, no résumé and a brand-new high school diploma. And she was perfectly aware that it was her voice that had landed her that position. That and her willingness to work for next to nothing, make coffee and double as the station's receptionist. Ten years later, her voice was hardly her only qualification. But it still often turned the tide.

She'd never found the time to pursue the degree in communications she still coveted. But she could double—and had—as engineer, newscaster, interviewer and program director. She had an encyclopedic memory for songs and recording artists, and a respect for both. Radio had been her home for a decade, and she loved it.

Her easygoing, flirtatious on-air personality was often at odds with the intense, organized and ambitious woman who rarely slept more than six hours and usually ate on the run. The public Cilla O'Roarke was a sexy radio princess who mingled with celebrities and had a job loaded with glamour and excitement. The private woman spent an average of ten hours a day at the station or on station business, was fiercely determined to put her younger sister through college and hadn't had a date in two years of Saturday nights.

And didn't want one.

Setting the headphones aside, she rechecked her daily log for her next fifteen-minute block. For the space of time it took to play a top 10 hit, the booth was silent. There was only Cilla and the lights and gauges on the control board. That was how she liked it best.

When she'd accepted the position with KHIP in Denver six months before, she'd wrangled for the 10:00-

p.m.-to-2-a.m. slot, one usually reserved for the novice deejay. A rising success with ten years experience behind her, she could have had one of the plum day spots when the listening audience was at its peak. She preferred the night, and for the past five years she'd carved out a name for herself in those lonely hours.

She liked being alone, and she liked sending her voice and music out to others who lived at night.

With an eye on the clock, Cilla adjusted her headphones. Between the fade-out of hit number four and the intro to hit number five, she crooned out the station's number four and the intro to hit number five, she crooned out the station's call letters and frequency. After a quick break when she popped in a cassette of recorded news, she would begin her favorite part of her show. The request line.

She enjoyed watching the phones light up, enjoyed hearing the voices. It took her out of her booth for fifty minutes every night and proved to her that there were people, real people with real lives, who were listening to her.

She lit a cigarette and leaned back in her swivel chair. This would be her last quiet moment for the next hour.

She didn't appear to be a restful woman. Nor, despite the voice, did she look like a smoldering femme fatale. There was too much energy in her face and in her long, nervous body for either. Her nails were unpainted, as was her mouth. She rarely found time in her schedule to bother with polish and paint. Her dark brandy-brown eyes were nearly closed as she allowed her body to charge up. Her lashes were long, an inheritance from her dreamy father. In contrast to the silky lashes and the pale, creamy complexion, her features were strong and angular. She had been blessed with a cloud of rich, wavy black hair that she ruthlessly pulled back, clipped back or twisted up in deference to the headphones.

With an eye on the elapsed-time clock, Cilla crushed out the cigarette and took a sip of water, then opened her mike. The On Air sign glowed green.

"That was for all the lovers out there, whether you've got someone to cuddle up with tonight or you wish you did. Stay tuned. This is Cilla O'Roarke, Denver. You're listening to KHIP. We're coming back with our request line."

As she switched on the tape for a commercial run, she glanced up. "Hey, Nick. How's it going?"

Nick Peters, the college student who served as an intern at the station, pushed up his dark-framed glasses and grinned. "I aced the Lit test."

"Way to go." She gratefully accepted the mug of steaming coffee he offered. "Is it still snowing?"

"Stopped about an hour ago."

She nodded and relaxed a little. She'd been worrying about Deborah, her younger sister. "I guess the roads are a mess."

"Not too bad. You want something to go with that coffee?"

She flicked him a smile, her mind too busy with other things to note the adoration in his eyes. "No, thanks. Help yourself to some stale doughnuts before you sign out." She hit a switch and spoke into the mike again.

As she read the station promos, he watched her. He knew it was hopeless, even stupid, but he was wildly in love with her. She was the most beautiful woman in the world to him, making the women at college look like awkward, gangling shadows of what a real woman should be. She was strong, successful, sexy. And she barely knew he was alive. When she noticed him at all, it was with a distractedly friendly smile or gesture.

For over three months he'd been screwing up his courage to ask her for a date. And fantasizing about what it would be like to have her attention focused on him, only him, for an entire evening.

She was completely unaware. Had she known where his mind had led him, Cilla would have been more amused than flattered. Nick was barely twenty-one, seven years her junior chronologically. And decades younger in every other way. She liked him. He was unobtrusive and efficient, and he wasn't afraid of long hours or hard work.

Over the past few months she'd come to depend on the coffee he brought her before he left the station. And to enjoy knowing she would be completely alone as she drank it.

Nick glanced at the clock. "I'll, ah, see you tomorrow."

"Hmm? Oh, sure. Good night, Nick." The moment he was through the door, she forgot about him. She punched one of the illuminated buttons on the phone. "KHIP. You're on the air."

"Cilla?"

"That's right. Who's this?"

"I'm Kate."

"Where are you calling from, Kate?"

"From home—over in Lakewood. My husband's a cab driver. He's working the late shift. We both listen to your show every night. Could you play 'Peaceful, Easy Feeling' for Kate and Ray?"

"You got it, Kate. Keep those home fires burning."
She punched the next button. "KHIP. You're on the
air."

The routine ran smoothly. Cilla would take calls,
scribbling down the titles and the dedications. The small
studio was lined with shelves crammed with albums,
45s, CDs, all labeled for easy access. After a handful of
calls she would break to commercials and station promos to give herself time to set up for the first block of
songs.

Some of the callers were repeaters, so she would chat
a moment or two. Some were the lonely, calling just to
hear the sound of another voice. Mixed in with them
was the occasional loony that she would joke off the line
or simply disconnect. In all her years of handling live
phones, she couldn't remember a moment's boredom.

She enjoyed it tremendously, chatting with callers,
joking. In the safety of the control booth she was able,
as she had never been able face-to-face, to relax and
develop an easy relationship with strangers. No one
hearing her voice would suspect that she was shy or insecure.

"KHIP. You're on the air."

"Cilla."

"Yes. You'll have to speak up, partner. What's your
name?"

"That doesn't matter."

"Okay, Mr. X." She rubbed suddenly damp palms on
the thighs of her jeans. Instinct told her she would have
trouble with this one, so she kept her finger hovering
over the seven-second-delay button. "You got a request?"

"I want you to pay, slut. I'm going to make you pay. When I'm finished, you're going to thank me for killing you. You're never going to forget."

Cilla froze, cursed herself for it, then cut him off in the midst of a rage of obscenities. Through strict control she kept her voice from shaking. "Wow. Sounds like somebody's a little cranky tonight. Listen, if that was Officer Marks, I'm going to pay those parking tickets. I swear. This one goes out to Joyce and Larry."

She shot in Springsteen's latest hit single, then sat back to remove the headphones with trembling hands.

Stupid. She rose to pluck out the next selection. After all these years she should have known better than to freak over a crank call. It was rare to get through a shift without at least one. She had learned to handle the odd, the angry, the propositions and the threats as skillfully as she had learned to handle the control board.

It was all part of the job, she reminded herself. Part of being a public personality, especially on the night shift, where the weird always got weirder.

But she caught herself glancing over her shoulder, through the dark glass of the studio to the dim corridor beyond. There were only shadows, and silence. Beneath her heavy sweater, her skin was shivering in a cold sweat. She was alone. Completely.

And the station's locked, she reminded herself as she cued up the next selection. The alarm was set. If it went off, Denver's finest would scream up to the station within minutes. She was as safe here as she would be in a bank vault.

But she stared down at the blinking lights on the phone, and she was afraid.

The snow had stopped, but its scent lingered in the chill March air. As she drove, Cilla kept the window down an inch and the radio up to the maximum. The combination of wind and music steadied her.

Cilla wasn't surprised to find that Deborah was waiting up for her. She pulled into the driveway of the house she'd bought only six months before and noted with both annoyance and relief that all the lights were blazing.

It was annoying because it meant Deborah was awake and worrying. And it was a relief, because the quiet suburban street seemed so deserted and she felt so vulnerable. She switched off the ignition, cutting the engine and the sounds of Jim Jackson's mellow all-night show. The instant of total silence had her heart leaping into her throat.

Swearing at herself, she slammed the car door and, hunched in her coat against the wind, dashed up the stairs. Deborah met her at the door.

"Hey, don't you have a nine-o'clock class tomorrow?" Stalling, Cilla peeled off her coat and hung it in the closet. She caught the scent of hot chocolate and furniture polish. It made her sigh. Deborah always resorted to housecleaning when she was tense. "What are you doing up at this hour?"

"I heard. Cilla, that man—"

"Oh, come on, baby." Turning, Cilla wrapped her arms around her sister. In her plain white terry-cloth robe, Deborah still seemed twelve years old to her. There was no one Cilla loved more. "Just one more harmless nut in a fruitcake world."

"He didn't sound harmless, Cilla." Though several inches shorter, Deborah held Cilla still. There was a resemblance between them—around the mouth. Both their mouths were full, passionate and stubborn. But Deborah's features were softer, curved rather than angular. Her eyes, thickly lashed, were a brilliant blue. They were drenched now with concern. "I think you should call the police."

"The police?" Because this option had simply not occurred to her, Cilla was able to laugh. "One obscene call and you have me dashing to the cops. What kind of nineties woman do you take me for?"

Deborah jammed her hands in her pockets. "This isn't a joke."

"Okay, it's not a joke. But Deb, we both know how little the police could do about one nasty call to a public radio station in the middle of the night."

With an impatient sigh, Deborah turned away. "He really sounded vicious. It scared me."

"Me too."

Deborah's laugh was quick, and only a little strained. "You're never scared."

I'm always scared, Cilla thought, but she smiled. "I was this time. It shook me enough that I fumbled the delay button and let it broadcast." Fleetingly she wondered how much flak she'd get for that little lapse the next day. "But he didn't call back, which proves it was a one-shot deal. Go to bed," she said, passing a hand over her sister's dark, fluffy hair. "You're never going to be the best lawyer in Colorado if you stay up pacing all night."

"I'll go if you go."

Knowing it would be hours before her mind and body settled down, Cilla draped an arm over her sister's shoulders. "It's a deal."

He kept the room dark, but for the light of a few sputtering candles. He liked the mystic, spiritual glow of them, and their dreamy religious scent. The room was small, but it was crammed with mementos—trophies from his past. Letters, snapshots, a scattering of small china animals, ribbons faded by time. A long-bladed hunting knife rested across his knees, gleaming dully in the shifting light. A well-oiled .45 automatic rested by his elbow on a starched crocheted doily.

In his hand he held a picture framed in rosewood. He stared at it, spoke to it, wept bitter tears over it. This was the only person he had ever loved, and all he had left was the picture to press to his breast.

John. Innocent, trusting John. Deceived by a woman. Used by a woman. Betrayed by a woman.

Love and hate entwined as he rocked. She would pay. She would pay the ultimate price. But first she would suffer.

The call—one single ugly call—came every night. By the end of a week, Cilla's nerves were frazzled. She wasn't able to make a joke of it, on or off the air. She was just grateful that now she had learned to recognize the voice, that harsh, wire-taut voice with that undercurrent of fury, and she would cut him off after the first few words.

Then she would sit there in terror at the knowledge that he would call back, that he was there, just on the other side of one of those blinking lights, waiting to torment her.

What had she done?

After she dropped in the canned news and commercial spots at 2:00 a.m., Cilla rested her elbows on the table and dropped her head into her hands. She rarely slept well or deeply, and in the past week she had managed only a few snatches of real sleep. It was beginning to tell, she knew, on her nerves, her concentration.

What had she done?

That question haunted her. What could she possibly have done to make someone hate her? She had recognized the hate in the voice, the deep-seated hate. She knew she could sometimes be abrupt and impatient with people. There were times when she was insensitive. But she had never deliberately hurt anyone. What was it she would have to pay for? What crime, real or imagined, had she committed that caused this person to focus in on her for revenge?

Out of the corner of her eye she saw a movement. A shadow amid the shadows in the corridor. Panic arrowed into her, and she sprang up, jarring her hip against the console. The voice she had disconnected barely ten minutes before echoed in her head. She watched, rigid with fright, as the knob on the studio door turned.

There was no escape. Dry-mouthed, she braced for a fight.

"Cilla?"

Heart thudding, she lowered slowly into her chair, cursing her own nerves. "Mark."

"Sorry, I must have scared you."

"Only to death." Making an effort, she smiled at the station manager. He was in his middle thirties, and he was drop-dead gorgeous. His dark hair was carefully styled and on the long side, adding more youth to his smooth and tanned face. As always, his attire was carefully hip. "What are you doing here at this hour?"

"It's time we did more than talk about these calls."

"We had a meeting just a couple of days ago. I told you—"

"You told me," he agreed. "You have a habit of telling me, and everybody else."

"I'm not taking a vacation." She spun around in her chair to face him. "I've got nowhere to go."

"Everybody's got somewhere to go." He held up a hand before she could speak. "I'm not going to argue about this anymore. I know it's a difficult concept for you, but I am the boss."

She tugged at the hem of her sweatshirt. "What are you going to do? Fire me?"

He didn't know that she held her breath on the challenge. Though he'd worked with her for months, he hadn't scratched deep enough beneath the surface to understand how precarious was her self-esteem. If he had threatened her then, she would have folded. But all he knew was that her show had pumped new life into the station. The ratings were soaring.

"That wouldn't do either of us any good." Even as she let out the pent-up breath, he laid a hand on her shoulder. "Look, I'm worried about you, Cilla. All of us are."

It touched her, and, as always, it surprised her. "All he does is talk." For now. Scooting her chair toward the turntables, she prepared for the next music sweep.

"I'm not going to stand by while one of my people is harassed. I've called the police."

She sprang up out of her chair. "Damn it, Mark. I told you—"

"You told me." He smiled. "Let's not go down that road again. You're an asset to the station. And I'd like to think we were friends."

She sat down again, kicking out her booted feet. "Sure. Hold on." Struggling to concentrate, she went on-air with a station plug and the intro for the upcoming song. She gestured toward the clock. "You've got three minutes and fifteen seconds to convince me."

"Very simply, Cilla, what this guy's doing is against the law. I should never have let you talk me into letting it go this long."

"If we ignore him, he'll go away."

"Your way isn't working." He dropped his hand onto her shoulder again, patiently kneading the tensed muscles there. "So we're going to try mine. You talk to the cops or you take an unscheduled vacation."

Defeated, she looked up and managed a smile. "Do you push your wife around this way?"

"All the time." He grinned, then leaned down to press a kiss on her brow. "She loves it."

"Excuse me."

Cilla jerked back in what she knew could easily be mistaken for guilt. The two people in the doorway of the booth studied her with what she recognized as professional detachment.

The woman looked like a fashion plate, with a flow of dark red hair cascading to her shoulders and small, elegant sapphires at her ears that matched her eyes. Her complexion was the delicate porcelain of a true redhead. She had a small, compact body and wore a neatly tailored suit in wild shades of blue and green.

The man beside her looked as if he'd just spent a month on the range driving cattle. His shaggy blond hair was sun-streaked and fell over the collar of a denim work shirt. His jeans were worn and low at the hips, snug over what looked to Cilla to be about three feet of leg. The hems were frayed. Lanky, he slouched in the doorway, while the woman stood at attention. His boots were scuffed, but he wore a classically cut tweed jacket over his scruffy shirt.

He didn't smile. Cilla found herself staring, studying his face longer than she should have. There were hollows beneath his cheekbones, and there was the faintest of clefts in his chin. His tanned skin was taut over his facial bones, and his mouth, still unsmiling, was wide and firm. His eyes, intent enough on her face to make her want to squirm, were a clear bottle green.

"Mr. Harrison." The woman spoke first. Cilla thought there was a flicker of amusement in her eyes as she stepped forward. "I hope we gave you enough time."

Cilla sent Mark a killing look. "You told me you'd called them. You didn't tell me they were waiting outside."

"Now you know." He kept a hand on her shoulder, but this time it was more restraining than comforting. "This is Ms. O'Roarke."

"I'm Detective Grayson. This is my partner, Detective Fletcher."

"Thank you again for waiting." Mark gestured her, then her partner, in. The man lazily unfolded himself from the doorjamb.

"Detective Fletcher and I are both used to it. We could use a bit more information."

"As you know, Ms. O'Roarke has been getting some disturbing calls here at the station."

"Cranks." Cilla spoke up, annoyed at being talked around. "Mark shouldn't have bothered you with it."

"We're paid to be bothered." Boyd Fletcher eased a lean hip down on the table. "So, this where you work?"

There was just enough insolence in his eyes to raise her hackles. "I bet you're a hell of a detective."

"Cilla." Tired and wishing he was home with his wife, Mark scowled at her. "Let's cooperate." Ignoring her, he turned to the detectives again. "The calls started during last Tuesday's show. None of us paid much attention, but they continued. The last one came in tonight, at 12:35."

"Do you have tapes?" Althea Grayson had already pulled out her notebook.

"I started making copies of them after the third call." At Cilla's startled look, Mark merely shrugged. "A precaution. I have them in my office."

Boyd nodded to Althea. "Go ahead. I'll take Ms. O'Roarke's statement."

"Cooperate," Mark said to Cilla, and led Althea out.

In the ensuing silence, Cilla tapped a cigarette out of her dwindling pack and lit it with quick, jerky movements. Boyd drew in the scent longingly. He'd quit only six weeks, three days and twelve hours ago.

"Slow death," he commented.

Cilla studied him through the haze of smoke. "You wanted a statement."

"Yeah." Curious, he reached over to toy with a switch. Automatically she batted his fingers aside.

"Hands off."

Boyd grinned. He had the distinct feeling that she was speaking of herself, as well as her equipment.

She cued up an established hit. After opening her mike, she did a backsell on the song just fading—the title, the artist, the station's call letters and her name. In an easy rhythm, she segued into the next selection. "Let's make it quick," she told him. "I don't like company during my shift."

"You're not exactly what I expected."

"I beg your pardon?"

No, indeed, he thought. She was a hell of a lot more than he'd expected. "I've caught your show," he said easily. "A few times." More than a few. He'd lost more than a few hours' sleep listening to that voice. Liquid sex. "I got this image, you know. Five-seven." He took a casual glance from the top of her head, down her body, to the toe of her boots. "I guess I was close there. But I took you for a blonde, hair down to your waist, blue eyes, lots of . . . personality." He grinned again, enjoying the annoyance in her eyes. Big brown eyes, he noted. Definitely different, and more appealing than his fantasy.

"Sorry to disappoint you."

"Didn't say I was disappointed."

She took a long, careful drag, then deliberately blew the smoke in his direction. If there was one thing she knew how to do, it was how to discourage an obnoxious male.

"Do you want a statement or not, Slick?"

"That's what I'm here for." He took a pad and the stub of a pencil out of his jacket pocket. "Shoot."

In clipped, dispassionate terms, she ran through every call, the times, the phrasing. She continued to work as she spoke, pushing in recorded tapes of commercials, cuing up a CD, replacing and selecting albums.

Boyd's brow rose as he wrote. He would check the tapes, of course, but he had the feeling that she was giving him word-for-word. In his job he respected a good memory.

"You've been in town, what? Six months?"

"More or less."

"Make any enemies?"

"A salesman trying to hawk encyclopedias. I slammed the door on his foot."

Boyd spared her a glance. She was trying to make light of it, but she had crushed out her cigarette and was now gnawing on her thumbnail. "Dump any lovers?"

"No."

"Have any?"

Temper flashed in her eyes again. "You're the detective. You find out."

"I would—if it was personal." His eyes lifted again in a look that was so direct, so completely personal, that her palms began to sweat. "Right now I'm just doing my job. Jealousy and rejection are powerful motivators. According to your statements, most of the comments he made to you had to do with your sexual habits."

Bluntness might be her strong suit, but she wasn't about to tell him that her only sexual habit was abstinence. "I'm not involved with anyone at the moment," she said evenly.

"Good." Without glancing up, he made another note. "That was a personal observation."

"Look, Detective—"

"Cool your jets, O'Roarke," he said mildly. "It was an observation, not a proposition." His dark, patient eyes took her measure. "I'm on duty. I need a list of the men you've had contact with on a personal level. We'll keep it to the past six months for now. You can leave out the door-to-door salesman."

"I'm not involved." Her hands clenched as she rose. "I haven't been involved. I've had no desire to be involved."

"No one ever said desire couldn't be one-sided." At the moment he was damn sure his was.

She was suddenly excruciatingly tired. Dragging a hand through her hair, she struggled for patience. "Anyone should be able to see that this guy is hung up on a voice over the radio. He doesn't even know me. He's probably never seen me. An image," she said, tossing his own words back at him. "That's all I am to him. In this business it happens all the time. I haven't done anything."

"I didn't say you had."

There was no teasing note in his voice now. The sudden gentleness in it had her spinning around, blinking furiously at threatening tears. Overworked, she told herself. Overstressed. Overeverything. With her back to him, she fought for control.

Tough, he thought. She was a tough lady. The way her hands balled at her sides as she fought with her emotions was much more appealing, much sexier, than broken sighs or helpless gestures could ever be.

He would have liked to go to her, to speak some word of comfort or reassurance, to stroke a hand down her hair. She'd probably bite it off at the wrist.

"I want you to think about the past few months, see if you can come up with anything, however small and unimportant, that might have led to this." His tone had changed again. It was brisk now, brisk and dispassionate. "We can't bring every man in the greater Denver area in for questioning. It doesn't work that way."

"I know how cops work."

The bitterness in her voice had his brows drawing together. There was something else here, but this wasn't the time to dig into it.

"You'd recognize the voice if you heard it again."

"Yes."

"Anything familiar about it?"

"Nothing."

"Do you think it was disguised?"

She moved her shoulders restlessly, but when she turned back to him she had herself under control. "He keeps it muffled and low. It's, ah . . . like a hiss."

"Any objections to me sitting in on tomorrow night's show."

Cilla took another long look at him. "Barrels of them."

He inclined his head. "I'll just go to your boss."

Disgusted, she reached for her cigarettes. He closed his firm hard-palmed hand over hers. She stared down at the tangled fingers, shocked to realize that her pulse had doubled at the contact.

"Let me do my job, Cilla. It'll be easier all around if you let Detective Grayson and me take over."

"Nobody takes over my life." She jerked her hand away, then jammed it into her pocket.

"Just this small part of it, then." Before she could stop him, he reached out and tucked her hair behind her ear. "Go home and get some sleep. You look beat."

She stepped back, made herself smile. "Thanks, Slick. I feel a lot better now."

Though she grumbled, she couldn't prevent him waiting until she signed off and turned the studio over to the all-night man. Nor did her lack of enthusiasm discourage him from walking her out to her car, reminding her to lock her door and waiting until she'd driven away. Disturbed by the way he'd looked at her—and the way she'd reacted—she watched him in the rearview mirror until he was out of sight.

"Just what I needed," she muttered to herself. "A cowboy cop."

Moments later, Althea joined Boyd in the parking lot. She had the tapes in her bag, along with Mark's statement. "Well, Fletcher—" she dropped a friendly hand on his shoulder "—what's the verdict?"

"She's tough as nails, hardheaded, prickly as a briar patch." With his hands in his pockets, he rocked back on his heels. "I guess it must be love."

# Chapter 2

She was good, Boyd thought as he downed his bitter coffee and watched Cilla work. She handled the control board with an automatic ease that spoke of long experience—switching to music, to recorded announcements, to her own mike. Her timing was perfect, her delivery smooth. And her fingernails were bitten to the quick.

She was a package full of nerves and hostility. The nerves she tried to hide. She didn't bother with the hostility. In the two hours they'd been in the booth together, she had barely spoken a word to him. A neat trick, since the room was barely ten by ten.

That was fine. As a cop, he was used to being where he wasn't wanted. And he was just contrary enough to enjoy it.

He liked his job. Things like annoyance, animosity and belligerence didn't concern him. The simple fact was that negative emotions were a whole lot easier to deal with than a .45 slug. He'd had the opportunity to be hit with both.

Though he would have been uncomfortable with the term philosopher, he had a habit of analyzing everything down to its most basic terms. A the root of this was an elemental belief in right and wrong. Or—though he would have hesitated to use the phrase—good and evil.

He was savvy enough to know that crime often did pay, and pay well. Satisfaction came from playing a part in seeing that it didn't pay for long. He was a patient man. If a perpetrator took six hours or six months to bring down, the results were exactly the same. The good guys won.

Stretching out his long legs, he continued to page through his book while Cilla's voice washed over him. Her voice made him think of porch swings, hot summer nights and the sound of a slow-moving river. In direct contrast was the tension and restless energy that vibrated from her. He was content to enjoy the first and wonder about the second.

He was driving her crazy. Just being there. Cilla switched to a commercial, checked her playlist and deliberately ignored him. Or tried to. She didn't like company in the booth. It didn't matter that when she had coolly discouraged conversation he had settled back with his book—not the Western or men's adventure she had expected, but a dog-eared copy of Steinbeck's *East of Eden*. It didn't matter that he had been patiently quiet for nearly two hours.

He was there. And that was enough.

She couldn't pretend that the calls had stopped, that they meant nothing, that her life was back on its normal track. Not with this lanky cowboy reading the great American novel in the corner of the booth, so that she had to all but climb over him to get to the albums stored on the back wall. He brought all her nerves swimming to the surface.

She resented him for that, for his intrusion, and for the simple fact that he was a cop.

But that was personal, she reminded herself. She had a job to do.

"That was INXS taking you to midnight. It's a new day, Denver. March 28, but we're not going out like a lamb. It's eighteen degrees out there at 12:02, so tune in and heat up. You're listening to KHIP, where you get more hits per hour. We've got the news coming up, then the request line. Light up those phones and we'll rock and roll."

Boyd waited until she'd run through the news and moved to a commercial before he marked his place in his book and rose. He could feel the tension thicken as he sat in the chair next to Cilla.

"I don't want you to cut him off."

She stiffened and struggled to keep her voice carelessly sarcastic. "My listeners don't tune in for that kind of show, Slick."

"You can keep him on the line, on the studio speakers, without sending it on air, right?"

"Yes, but I don't want to—"

"Cut to a commercial or some music," Boyd said mildly, "but keep him on the line. We might get lucky and trace the call."

Her hands were balled into fists in her lap as she stared at the lights that were already blinking on the phone. He was right. She knew he was right. And she hated it.

"This is an awful lot of trouble for one loose screw."

"Don't worry." He smiled a little. "I get paid the same whether the screws are loose or tight."

She glanced down at the clock, cleared her throat, then switched on her mike. "Hello, Denver, this is Cilla O'Roarke for KHIP. You're listening to the hottest station in the Rockies. This is your chance to make it even hotter. Our request lines are open. I'll be playing what you want to hear, so give me a call at 555-KHIP. That's 555-5447."

Her finger trembled slightly as she punched the first lit button.

"This is Cilla O'Roarke. You're on the air."

"Hi, Cilla, this is Bob down in Englewood."

She closed her eyes on a shudder of relief. He was a regular. "Hey, Bob. How's it going?"

"Going great. My wife and I are celebrating our fifteenth anniversary tonight."

"And they said it wouldn't last. What can I play for you, Bob?"

"How about 'Cherish' for Nancy from Bob."

"Nice choice. Here's to fifteen more, Bob."

With her pen in one hand, she took the second call, then the third. Boyd watched her tighten up after each one. She chatted and joked. And grew paler. At the first break, she pulled a cigarette out of the pack, then fumbled with a match. Silently Boyd took the matches from her and lit one for her.

"You're doing fine."

She took a quick, jerky puff. Patient, he waited in silence for her to respond. "Do you have to watch me?"

"No." Then he smiled. It was a long, lazy smile that had her responding in spite of herself. "A man's entitled to some fringe benefits."

"If this is the best you can do, Slick, you ought to look for another line of work."

"I like this one." He rested the ankle of his boot on his knee. "I like it fine."

It was easier, Cilla decided, to talk to him than to stare at the blinking lights on the phone and worry. "Have you been a cop long?"

"Going on ten years."

She looked at him then, struggling to relax by concentrating on his face. He had calm eyes, she thought. Dark and calm. Eyes that had seen a lot and learned to live with it. There was a quiet kind of strength there, the kind women—some women—were drawn to. He would protect and defend. He wouldn't start a fight. But he would finish one.

Annoyed with herself, she looked away again, busying herself with her notes. She didn't need to be protected or defended. She certainly didn't need anyone to fight for her. She had always taken care of herself. And she always would.

"It's a lousy job," she said. "Being a cop."

He shifted. His knee brushed her thigh. "Mostly."

Instinctively she jiggled her chair for another inch of distance. "It's hard to figure why anyone would stick with a lousy job for ten years."

He just grinned. "I guess I'm in a rut."

She shrugged, then turned to her mike. "That was for Bill and Maxine. It's 12:20, and our request lines are still open. That's 555-5447." After one quick breath, she punched a button. "KHIP. You're on the air."

It went smoothly, so smoothly that she began to relax. She took call after call, falling into her old, established rhythm. Gradually she began to enjoy the music again, the flow of it. The pulsing lights on the phone no longer seemed threatening. By 12:45 she was sure she was going to make it through.

Just one night, she told herself. If he didn't call tonight, it would be over. She looked at the clock, watched the seconds tick by. Eight more minutes to go and she would turn the airwaves over to Jackson. She would go home, take a long, hot bath and sleep like a baby.

"KHIP, you're on the air."

"Cilla."

The hissing whisper shot ice through her veins. She reached over reflexively to disconnect, but Boyd clamped a hand over her wrist and shook his head. For a moment she struggled, biting back panic. His hand remained firm on hers, his eyes calm and steady.

Boyd watched as she fought for control, until she jammed in a cassette of commercials. The bright, bouncy jingles transmitted as she put the call on the studio speaker.

"Yes." Pride made her keep her eyes on Boyd's. "This is Cilla. What do you want?"

"Justice. I only want justice."

"For what?"

"I want you to think about that. I want you to think and wonder and sweat until I come for you."

**Journey with Harlequin into the past and discover stories of cowboys and captains, pirates and princes in the romantic tradition of Harlequin.**

Printed in Canada

"Why?" Her hand flexed under Boyd's. In an instinctive gesture of reassurance, he linked his fingers with hers. "Who are you?"

"Who am I?" There was a laugh that skidded along her skin. "I'm your shadow, your conscience. Your executioner. You have to die. When you understand, only when you understand, I'll end it. But it won't be quick. It won't be easy. You're going to pay for what you've done."

"What have I done?" she shouted. "For God's sake, what have I done?"

He spit out a stream of obscenities that left her dazed and nauseated before he broke the connection. With one hand still covering hers, Boyd punched out a number on the phone.

"You get the trace?" he demanded, then bit off an oath. "Yeah. Right." Disgusted, he replaced the receiver. "Not long enough." He reached up to touch Cilla's pale cheek. "You okay?"

She could hardly hear him for the buzzing in her ears, but she nodded. Mechanically she turned to her mike, waiting until the commercial jingle faded.

"That about wraps it up for this morning. It's 1:57. Tina Turner's going to rock you through until two. My man Jackson's coming it to keep all you insomniacs company until 6:00 a.m. This is Cilla O'Roarke for KHIP. Remember, darling, when you dream of me, dream good."

Light-headed, she pushed away from the console. She only had to stand up, she told herself. Walk to her car, drive home. It was simple enough. She did it every morning of her life. But she sat where she was, afraid her legs would buckle.

Jackson pushed through the door and stood there, hesitating. He was wearing a baseball cap to cover his healing hair transplant. "Hey, Cilla." He glanced from her to Boyd and back again. "Rough night, huh?"

Cilla braced herself, pasted on a careless smile. "I've had better." With every muscle tensed, she shoved herself to her feet. "I've got them warmed up for you, Jackson."

"Take it easy, kid."

"Sure." The buzzing in her ears was louder as she walked from the booth to snatch her coat from the rack. The corridors were dark, catching only a faint glow from the lobby, where the security lights burned. Disoriented, she blinked. She didn't even notice when Boyd took her arm and led her outside.

The cold air helped. She took big, thirsty gulps of it, releasing it again in thin plumes of white smoke. "My car's over there," she said when Boyd began to pull her toward the opposite end of the lot.

"You're in no shape to drive."

"I'm fine."

"Great. Then we'll go dancing."

"Look—"

"No, you look." He was angry, furious. He hadn't realized it himself until that moment. She was shaking, and despite the chill wind her cheeks were deadly pale. Listening to the tapes hadn't been the same as being there when the call came through, seeing the blood drain out of her face and her eyes glaze with terror. And not being able to do a damn thing to stop it. "You're a mess, O'Roarke, and I'm not letting you get behind the wheel of a car." He stopped next to his car and yanked open the door. "Get in. I'll take you home."

She tossed the hair out of her eyes. "Serve and protect, right?"

"You got it. Now get in before I arrest you for loitering."

Because her knees felt like jelly, she gave in. She wanted to be asleep, alone in some small, quiet room. She wanted to scream. Worse, she wanted to cry. Instead, she rounded on Boyd the second he settled in the driver's seat.

"You know what I hate even more than cops?"

He turned the key in the ignition. "I figure you're going to tell me."

"Men who order women around just because they're men. I don't figure that as a cultural hang-up, just stupidity. The way I look at it, that's two counts against you, Detective."

He leaned over, deliberately crowding her back in her seat. He got a moment's intense satisfaction out of seeing her eyes widen in surprise, her lips part on a strangled protest. The satisfaction would have been greater, he knew, if he had gone on impulse and covered that stubborn, sassy mouth with his own. He was certain she would taste exactly as she sounded—hot, sexy and dangerous.

Instead, he yanked her seat belt around her and fastened it.

Her breath came out in a whoosh when he took the wheel again. It had been a rough night, Cilla reminded herself. A tense, disturbing and unsettling night. Otherwise she would never have sat like a fool and allowed herself to be intimidated by some modern-day cowboy.

Her hands were shaking again. The reason didn't seem to matter, only the weakness.

"I don't think I like your style, Slick."

"You don't have to." She was getting under his skin, Boyd realized as he turned out of the lot. That was always a mistake. "Do what you're told and we'll get along fine."

"I don't do what I'm told," she snapped. "And I don't need a second-rate cop with a John Wayne complex to give me orders. Mark's the one who called you in, not me. I don't need you and I don't want you."

He braked at a light. "Tough."

"If you think I'm going to fall apart because some creep calls me names and makes threats, you're wrong."

"I don't think you're going to fall apart, O'Roarke, any more than you think I'm going to pick up the pieces if you do."

"Good. Great. I can handle him all by myself, and if you get your kicks out of listening to that kind of garbage—" She broke off, appalled with herself. Lifting her hands, she pressed them to her face and took three deep breaths.

"I'm sorry."

"For?"

"For taking it out on you." She dropped her hands into her lap and stared at them. "Could you pull over for a minute?"

Without a word, he guided the car to the curb and stopped.

"I want to calm down before I get home." In a deliberate effort to relax, she let her head fall back and her eyes close. "I don't want to upset my sister."

It was hard to hold on to rage and resentment when the woman sitting next to him had turned from barbed wire to fragile glass. But if his instincts about Cilla were on target, too much sympathy would set her off again.

"Want some coffee?"

"No thanks." The corners of her mouth turned up for the briefest instant. "I've poured in enough to fuel an SST." She let out a long, cleansing breath. The giddiness was gone, and with it that floating sense of unreality. "I am sorry, Slick. You're only doing your job."

"You got that right. Why do you call me Slick?"

She opened her eyes, made a brief but comprehensive study of his face. "Because you are." Turning away, she dug in her bag for a cigarette. "I'm scared." She hated the fact that the admission was shaky, that her hand was unsteady as she struck a match.

"You're entitled."

"No, I'm really scared." She let out smoke slowly, watching a late-model sedan breeze down the road and into the night. "He wants to kill me. I didn't really believe that until tonight." She shuddered. "Is there any heat in this thing?"

He turned the fan on full. "It's better if you're scared."

"Why?"

"You'll cooperate."

She smiled. It was a full flash of a smile that almost stopped his heart. "No, I won't. This is only a momentary respite. I'll be giving you a hard time as soon as I recover."

"I'll try not to get used to this." But it would be easy, he realized, to get used to the way her eyes warmed when she smiled. The way her voice eased over a man and made him wonder. "Feeling better?"

"Lots. Thanks." She tapped out her cigarette as he guided the car back on the road. "I take it you know where I live."

"That's why I'm a detective."

"It's a thankless job." She pushed her hair back from her forehead. They would talk, she decided. Just talk. Then she wouldn't have to think. "Why aren't you out roping cattle or branding bulls? You've got the looks for it."

He considered a moment. "I'm not sure that's a compliment, either."

"You're fast on the draw, Slick."

"Boyd," he said. "It wouldn't hurt you to use my name." When she only shrugged, he slanted her a curious look. "Cilla. That'd be from Priscilla, right?"

"No one calls me Priscilla more than once."

"Why?"

She sent him her sweetest smile. "Because I cut out their tongues."

"Right. You want to tell me why you don't like cops?"

"No." She turned away to stare out the side window. "I like the nighttime," she said, almost to herself. "You can do things, say things, at three o'clock in the morning that it's just not possible to do or say at three o'clock in the afternoon. I can't even imagine what it's like to work in the daylight anymore, when people are crowding the air."

"You don't like people much, do you?"

"Some people." She didn't want to talk about herself, her likes and dislikes, her successes, her failures.

She wanted to talk about him—to satisfy her curiosity, and to ease her jangled nerves. "So, how long have you had the night shift, Fletcher?"

"About nine months." He glanced at her. "You meet an . . . interesting class of people."

She laughed, surprised that she was able to. "Don't you just? Are you from Denver?"

"Born and bred."

"I like it," she said, surprising herself again. She hadn't given it a great deal of thought. It had simply been a place that offered a good college for Deborah and a good opportunity for her. Yet in six months, she realized, she had come close to sinking roots. Shallow ones, but roots nonetheless.

"Does that mean you're going to stick around?" He turned down a quiet side street. "I did some research. It seems two years in one spot's about your limit."

"I like change," she said flatly, closing down the lines of communication. She didn't care for the idea of anyone poking into her past and her private life. When he pulled up in her driveway, she was already unsnapping her seat belt. "Thanks for the ride, Slick."

Before she could dash to her door, he was beside her. "I'm going to need your keys."

They were already in her hand. She clutched them possessively. "Why?"

"So I can have your car dropped off in the morning."

She jingled them, frowning, as she stood under the front porch light. Boyd wondered what it would be like to walk her to her door after an ordinary date. He wouldn't keep his hands in his pockets, he thought ruefully. And he certainly would scratch this itch by kissing her outside the door.

Outside, hell, he admitted. He would have been through the door with her. And there would have been more to the end of the evening than a good-night kiss.

But it wasn't a date. And any fool could see that there wasn't going to be anything remotely ordinary between them. Something. That he promised himself. But nothing remotely resembling the ordinary.

"Keys?" he repeated.

After going over her options, Cilla had decided his was best. Carefully she removed a single key from the chain, which was shaped like a huge musical note. "Thanks."

"Hold it." He placed the palm of his hand on the door as she unlocked it. "You're not going to ask me in for a cup of coffee?"

She didn't turn, only twisted her head. "No."

She smelled like the night, he thought. Dark, deep, dangerous. "That's downright unfriendly."

The flash of humor came again. "I know. See you around, Slick."

His hand dropped onto hers on the knob, took a firm hold. "Do you eat?"

The humor vanished. That didn't surprise him. What did was what replaced it. Confusion. And—he could have sworn—shyness. She recovered so quickly that he was certain he'd imagined it.

"Once or twice a week."

"Tomorrow." His hand remained over hers. He couldn't be sure about what he'd thought he saw in her eyes, but he knew her pulse had quickened under his fingers.

"I may eat tomorrow."

"With me."

It amazed her that she fumbled. It had been years since she'd experienced this baffling reaction to a man. And those years had been quiet and smooth. Refusing a date was as simple as saying no. At least it always had been for her. Now she found herself wanting to smile and ask him what time she should be ready. The words were nearly out of her mouth before she caught herself.

"That's an incredibly smooth offer, Detective, but I'll have to pass."

"Why?"

"I don't date cops."

Before she could weaken, she slipped inside and closed the door in his face.

Boyd shuffled the papers on his desk and scowled. The O'Roarke case was hardly his only assignment, but he couldn't get his mind off it. Couldn't get his mind off O'Roarke, he thought, wishing briefly but intensely for a cigarette.

The veteran cop sitting two feet away from him was puffing away like a chimney as he talked to a snitch. Boyd breathed in deep, wishing he could learn to hate the smell like other nonsmokers.

Instead, he continued to torture himself by drawing in the seductive scent—that, and the other, less appealing aromas of a precinct station. Overheated coffee, overheated flesh, the cheap perfume hovering around a pair of working girls who lounged resignedly on a nearby bench.

Intrusions, he thought, that he rarely noticed in the day-to-day scheme of things. Tonight they warred with his concentration. The smells, the sound of keyboards clicking, phones ringing, shoes scuffing along the linoleum, the way one of the overhead lights winked sporadically.

It didn't help his disposition that for the past three days Priscilla Alice O'Roarke had stuck fast to his mind like a thick, thorny spike. No amount of effort could shake her loose. It might be because both he and his partner had spent hours at a time with her in the booth during her show. It might be because he'd seen her with her defenses down. It might be because he'd felt, fleetingly, her surge of response to him.

It might be, Boyd thought in disgust. Then again, it might not.

He wasn't a man whose ego was easily bruised by the refusal of a date. He liked to think that he had enough confidence in himself to understand he didn't appeal to every woman. The fact that he'd appealed to what he considered a healthy number of them in his thirty-three years was enough to satisfy him.

The trouble was, he was hung up on one woman. And she wasn't having any of it.

He could live with it.

The simple fact was that he had a job to do now. He wasn't convinced that Cilla was in any immediate danger. But she was being harassed, systematically and thoroughly. Both he and Althea had started the ball rolling, questioning men with priors that fit the M.O., poking their fingers into Cilla's personal and professional life since she had come to Denver, quietly investigating her co-workers.

So far the score was zip.

Time to dig deeper, Boyd decided. He had Cilla's résumé in his hand. It was an interesting piece of work in itself. Just like the woman it belonged to. It showed her bouncing from a one-horse station in Georgia—which accounted for that faint and fascinating Southern drawl—to a major player in Atlanta, then on to Richmond, St. Louis, Chicago, before landing—feet first, obviously—in Denver at KHIP.

The lady likes to move, he mused. Or was it that she needed to run? That was a question of semantics, and he intended to get the answer straight from the horse's mouth.

The one thing he could be sure of from the bald facts typed out in front of him was that Cilla had pulled herself along the road to success with a high school diploma and a lot of guts. It couldn't have been easy for a woman—a girl, really, at eighteen—to break into what was still a largely male-dominated business.

"Interesting reading?" Althea settled a hip on the corner of his desk. No one in the station house would have dared whistle at her legs. But plenty of them looked.

"Cilla O'Roarke." He tossed the résumé down. "Impressions?"

"Tough lady." She grinned as she said it. She'd spent a lot of time razzing Boyd about his fascination with the sultry voice on the radio. "Likes to do things her own way. Smart and professional."

He picked up a box of candy-coated almonds and shook some into his hand. "I think I figured all that out myself."

"Well, figure this." Althea took the box and carefully selected one glossy nut. "She's scared down to the bone. And she's got an inferiority complex a mile wide."

"Inferiority complex." Boyd gave a quick snort and kicked back in his chair. "Not a chance."

With the same careful deliberation, Althea chose another candied almond. "She hides it behind three feet of steel, but it's there." Althea laid a hand on the toe of his boot. "Woman's intuition, Fletcher. That's why you're so damn lucky to have me."

Boyd snatched the box back, knowing Althea could, and would, methodically work her way through to the last piece. "If that woman's insecure, I'll eat my hat."

"You don't have a hat."

"I'll get one and eat it." Dismissing his partner's instincts, he gestured toward the files. "Since our man isn't letting up, we're going to have to go looking elsewhere for him."

"The lady isn't very forthcoming about her past."

"So we push."

Althea considered a moment. Then she shifted her weight gracefully, recrossed her legs. "Want to flip a coin? Because the odds are she'll push back."

Boyd grinned. "I'm counting on it."

"It's your turn in the booth tonight."

"Then you start with Chicago." He handed her the file. "We got the station manager, the landlord." He scanned the sheet himself. He intended to go far beyond what was printed there, but he would start with the facts. "Use that sweet, persuasive voice of yours. They'll spill their guts."

"Thousands have." She glanced over idly as an associate shoved a swearing suspect with a bloody nose into a nearby chair. There was a brief tussle, and a spate of curses followed by mumbled threats. "God, I love this place."

"Yeah, there's no place like home." He snatched up what was left of his coffee before his partner could reach for it. "I'll work from the other end, the first station she worked for. Thea, if we don't come up with something soon, the captain's going to yank us."

She rose. "Then we'll have to come up with something."

He nodded. Before he could pick up the phone, it rang. "Fletcher."

"Slick."

He would have grimaced at the nickname if he hadn't heard the fear first. "Cilla? What is it?"

"I got a call." A quick bubble of laughter worked its way through. "Old news, I guess. I'm at home this time, though, and I— Damn, I'm jumping at shadows."

"Lock your doors and sit tight. I'm on my way. Cilla," he said when there was no response. "I'm on my way."

"Thanks. If you could break a few traffic laws getting here, I'd be obliged."

"Ten minutes." He hung up. "Thea." He caught her before she could complete the first call. "Let's move."

# Chapter 3

She had herself under control by the time they got to her. Above all, she felt foolish to have run to the police—to him—because of a phone call.

Only phone calls, Cilla assured herself as she paced to the window and back. After a week of them she should have a better handle on it. If she could tone down her reaction, convince the caller that what he said and how he said it left her unaffected, they would stop.

Her father had taught her that that was the way to handle bullies. Then again, her mother's solution had been a right jab straight to the jaw. While Cilla saw value in both viewpoints, she thought the passive approach was more workable under the circumstances.

She'd done a lousy job of it with the last call, she admitted. Sometime during his tirade she'd come uncomfortably close to hysteria, shouting back, pleading, meeting threats with threats. She could only be grateful that Deborah hadn't been home to hear it.

Struggling for calm, she perched on the arm of a chair, her body ruler-straight, her mind scrambling. After the call she had turned off the radio, locked the doors, pulled the drapes. Now, in the glow of the lamplight, she sat listening for a sound, any sound, while she scanned the room. The walls she and Deborah had painted, the furniture they had picked out, argued about. Familiar things, Cilla thought. Calming things.

After only six months there was already a scattering of knickknacks, something they hadn't allowed themselves before. But this time the house wasn't rented, the furniture wasn't leased. It was theirs.

Perhaps that was why, though they'd never discussed it, they had begun to fill it with little things, useless things. The china cat who curled in a permanent nap on the cluttered bookshelf. The foolishly expensive glossy white bowl with hibiscus blossoms painted on the rim. The dapper frog in black tie and tails.

They were making a home, Cilla realized. For the first time since they had found themselves alone, they were making a home. She wouldn't let some vicious, faceless voice over the phone spoil that.

What was she going to do? Because she was alone, she allowed herself a moment of despair and dropped her head into her hands. Should she fight back? But how could she fight someone she couldn't see and didn't understand? Should she pretend indifference? But how long could she keep up that kind of pretense, especially if he continued to invade her private hours, as well as her public ones?

And what would happen when he finally wearied of talk and came to her in person?

The brisk knock on the door had her jolting, had her pressing a hand between her breasts to hold in her suddenly frantic heart.

*I'm your executioner. I'm going to make you suffer. I'm going to make you pay.*

"Cilla. It's Boyd. Open the door."

She needed a moment more, needed to cover her face with her hands and breathe deep. Steadier now, she crossed to the door and opened it.

"Hi. You made good time." She nodded to Althea. "Detective Grayson." Cilla gestured them inside, then leaned her back against the closed door. "I feel stupid for calling you all the way out here."

"Just part of the job," Althea told her. The woman was held together by very thin wires, she decided. A few of them had already snapped. "Would you mind if we all sat down?"

"No. I'm sorry." Cilla dragged a hand through her hair. She wasn't putting on a very good show, she thought. And she prided herself on putting on a good show. "I could, ah, make some coffee."

"Don't worry about it." He sat on an oatmeal-colored couch and leaned back against sapphire-blue pillows. "Tell us what happened."

"I wrote it down." The underlying nerves showed in her movements as she walked to the phone to pick up a pad of paper. "A radio habit," she said. "The phone rings and I start writing." She wasn't ready to admit that she didn't want to repeat the conversation out loud.

"Some of it's in O'Roarke shorthand, but you should get the drift."

He took the pad from her and scanned the words. His gut muscles tightened in a combination of fury and revulsion. Outwardly calm, he handed the note to his partner.

Cilla couldn't sit. Instead, she stood in the center of the room, twisting her fingers together, dragging them apart again to tug at her baggy sweatshirt. "He's pretty explicit about what he thinks of me, and what he intends to do about it."

"Is this your first call at home?" Boyd asked her.

"Yes. I don't know how he got the number. I— We're not listed."

Althea put the pad aside and took out her own. "Who has your home number?"

"The station." Cilla relaxed fractionally. This was something she could deal with. Simple questions, simple answers. "It would be on file at the college. My lawyer—that's Carl Donnely, downtown. There are a couple of guys that Deb sees. Josh Holden and Darren McKinley. A few girlfriends." She ran through the brief list. "That's about it. What I'm really concerned about is—" She spun around as the door opened behind her. "Deb." Relief and annoyance speared through her. "I thought you had evening classes."

"I did." She turned a pair of big, smoldering blue eyes on Boyd and Althea. "Are you the police?"

"Deborah," Cilla said, "you know better than to cut classes. You had a test—"

"Stop treating me like a child." She slapped the newspaper she was carrying into Cilla's hand. "Do you really expect me to go along like nothing's wrong? Damn it, Cilla, you told me it was all under control.''

So she'd made the first page of section B, Cilla thought wearily. Late-night radio princess under siege. Trying to soothe a growing tension headache, she rubbed her fingers at her temple. "It is under control. Stuff like this makes good copy, that's all."

"No, that's not all."

"I've called the police," she snapped back as she tossed the paper aside. "What else do you want?"

There was a resemblance between the two, Boyd noted objectively. The shape of the mouth and eyes. While Cilla was alluring and sexy enough to make a man's head turn a 360, her sister was hands-down gorgeous. Young, he thought. Maybe eighteen. In a few years she'd barely have to glance at a man to have him swallow his tongue.

He also noted the contrasts. Deborah's hair was short and fluffed. Cilla's was long and untamed. The younger sister wore a deep crimson sweater over tailored slacks that were tucked into glossy half boots. Cilla's mismatched sweats bagged and hit on a variety of colors. The top was purple, the bottoms green. She'd chosen thick yellow socks and orange high-tops.

Their tastes might clash, he mused, but their temperaments seemed very much in tune.

And when the O'Roarke sisters were in a temper, it was quite a show.

Shifting only slightly, Althea whispered near his ear. "Obviously they've done this before."

Boyd grinned. If he'd had popcorn and a beer, he would have been content to sit through another ten rounds. "Who's your money on?"

"Cilla," she murmured, crossing one smooth leg. "But the sister's a real up-and-comer."

Apparently weary of beating her head against a brick wall, Deborah turned. "Okay." She poked a finger at Boyd. "You tell me what's going on."

"Ah . . ."

"Never mind." She zeroed in on Althea. "You."

Biting back a smile, Althea nodded. "We're the investigating officers on your sister's case, Miss O'Roarke."

"So there is a case."

Ignoring Cilla's furious look, Althea nodded again. "Yes. With the station's cooperation, we have a trace on the studio line. Detective Fletcher and I have already interrogated a number of suspects who have priors for obscene or harassing phone calls. With this latest development, we'll put a tap on your private line."

"Latest development." It only took Deborah a moment. "Oh, Cilla, not here. He didn't call you here." Temper forgotten, she threw her arms around her sister. "I'm sorry."

"It's nothing for you to worry about." When Deborah stiffened, Cilla drew back. "I mean it, Deb. It's nothing for either of us to worry about. We've got the pros to do the worrying."

"That's right." Althea rose. "Detective Fletcher and I have over fifteen years on the force between us. We intend to take good care of your sister. Is there a phone I can use to make some arrangements?"

"In the kitchen," Deborah said before Cilla could comment. She wanted a private interview. "I'll show you." She paused and smiled at Boyd. "Would you like some coffee, Detective?"

"Thanks." He watched her—what man wouldn't?—as she walked from the room.

"Don't even think about it," Cilla mumbled.

"Excuse me?" But he grinned. It didn't take a detective to recognize a mother hen. "Your sister—Deborah, right?—she's something."

"You're too old for her."

"Ouch."

Cilla picked up a cigarette and forced herself to settle on the arm of a chair again. "In any case, you and Detective Grayson seem well suited to each other."

"Thea?" He had to grin again. Most of the time he forgot his partner was a woman. "Yeah, I'm one lucky guy."

Cilla ground her teeth. She hated to think she could be intimidated by another woman. Althea Grayson was personable enough, professional enough. Cilla could even handle the fact that she was stunning. It was just that she was so *together*.

Boyd rose to take the unlit cigarette from her fingers. "Jealous?"

"In your dreams, Slick."

"We'll get into my dreams later." He lifted her chin up with a fingertip. "Holding on?"

"I'm fine." She wanted to move, but she had the feeling he wouldn't give her room if she stood. And if she stood it would be much too easy to drop her head on his shoulder and just cave in. She had responsibilities, obligations. And her pride. "I don't want Deb mixed up in this. She's alone here at night while I'm at work."

"I can arrange to have a cruiser stationed outside."

She nodded, grateful. "I hate it that somewhere along the line I've made a mistake that might put her in danger. She doesn't deserve it."

Unable to resist, he spread his fingers to cup her cheek. "Neither do you."

It had been a long time since she'd been touched, allowed herself to be touched, even that casually. She managed to shrug. "I haven't figured that out yet." She gave a little sigh, wishing she could close her eyes and turn her face into that strong, capable hand. "I've got to get ready to go to the station."

"Why don't you give that a pass tonight?"

"And let him think he's got me running scared?" She stood then. "Not on a bet."

"Even Wonder Woman takes a night off."

She shook her head. She'd been right about him not giving her room. Her escape routes were blocked by the chair on one side and his body on the other. Tension quivered through her. Pride kept her eyes level. He was waiting, damn him. And unless he was blind or stupid he would see that this contact, this connection with him, left her frazzled.

"You're crowding me, Fletcher."

In another minute, just one more minute, he would have given in to impulse and pulled her against him. He would have seen just how close to reality his fantasy was. "I haven't begun to crowd you, O'Roarke."

Her eyes sharpened. "I've had enough threats for one day, thanks."

He wanted to strangle her for that. Slowly, his eyes on hers, he hooked his thumbs in his pockets. "No threat, babe. Just a fact."

Deborah decided she'd eavesdropped long enough and cleared her throat. "Coffee, Detective Fletcher." She passed him a steaming mug. "Thea said black, two sugars."

"Thanks."

"I'm going to hang around," she said, silently daring Cilla to argue with her. "They should be here in an hour or so to hook up the phone." Then, she put her hands on Cilla's shoulders and kissed both of her cheeks. "I haven't missed a class this semester, Simon."

"Simon?" Boyd commented.

"Legree." With a laugh, Deborah kissed Cilla again. "The woman's a slave driver."

"I don't know what you're talking about." Cilla moved aside to gather up her purse. "You ought to catch up on your reading for U.S. studies. Your political science could use a boost. It wouldn't hurt to bone up on Psychology 101." She pulled her coat from the closet. "While you're at it, the kitchen floor needs scrubbing. I'm sure we have an extra toothbrush you could use on it. And I'd like another cord of wood chopped."

Deborah laughed. "Go away."

Cilla grinned as she reached for the doorknob. Her hand closed over Boyd's. She jolted back before she could stop herself. "What are you doing?"

"Hitching a ride with you." He sent Deborah a quick wink as he pulled Cilla out the door.

"This is ridiculous," Cilla said as she strode into the station.

"Which?"

"I don't see why I have to have a cop in the studio with me night after night." She whipped off her coat as she walked—a bit like a bullfighter swirling a cape, Boyd thought. Still scowling, she reached for the door of a small storage room, then shrieked and stumbled back against Boyd as it swung open. "Jeez, Billy, you scared the life out of me."

"Sorry." The maintenance man had graying hair, toothpick arms and an apologetic grin. "I was out of window cleaner." He held up his spray bottle.

"It's okay. I'm a little jumpy."

"I heard about it." He hooked the trigger of the bottle in his belt, then gathered up a mop and bucket. "Don't worry, Cilla. I'm here till midnight."

"Thanks. Are you going to listen to the show tonight?"

"You bet." He walked away, favoring his right leg in a slight limp.

Cilla stepped inside the room and located a fresh bottle of stylus cleaner. Taking a five-dollar bill out of her bag, she slipped it into a pile of cleaning rags.

"What was that for?"

"He was in Vietnam," she said simply, and closed the door again.

Boyd said nothing, knowing she was annoyed he'd caught her. He chalked it up to one more contradiction.

To prep for her shift, she went into a small lounge to run over the daily log for her show, adding and deleting as it suited her. The program director had stopped screaming about this particular habit months before. Another reason she preferred the night shift was the leeway it gave her.

"This new group," she muttered.

"What?" Boyd helped himself to a sugared doughnut.

"This new group, the Studs." She tapped her pencil against the table. "One-shot deal. Hardly worth the airtime."

"Then why play them?"

"Got to give them a fair shake." Intent on her work, she took an absent bite of the doughnut Boyd held to her lips. "In six months nobody will remember their names."

"That's rock and roll."

"No. The Beatles, Buddy Holly, Chuck Berry, Springsteen, Elvis—that's rock and roll."

He leaned back, considering her. "Ever listen to anything else?"

She grinned, then licked a speck of sugar from her top lip. "You mean there *is* something else?"

"Have you always been one-track?"

"Yeah." She pulled a band of fabric out of her pocket. With a couple of flicks of the wrist she had her hair tied back. "So what kind of music do you like?"

"The Beatles, Buddy Holly, Chuck—"

"Well, there's hope for you yet," she interrupted.

"Mozart, Lena Horne, Beaujolais, Joan Jett, Ella Fitzgerald, B.B. King . . ."

Her brow lifted. "So, we're eclectic."

"We're open-minded."

She leaned back a moment. "You're a surprise, Fletcher. I guess I figured you for the loving-and-hurting, drinking-and-cheating type."

"In music appreciation or personality?"

"Both." She glanced at the clock. "It's show time."

Wild Bob Williams, who had the six-to-ten slot, was just finishing up his show. He was short, paunchy and middle-aged, with the voice of a twenty-year-old stud. He gave Cilla a brief salute as she began sorting through 45s and albums.

"Mmm, the long-legged filly just walked in." He hit a switch that had an echoing heartbeat pounding. "Get ready out there in KHIP land, your midnight star's rising. I'm leaving you with this blast from the past." He potted up "Honky Tonk Woman."

He swung out of his chair and stretched his rubbery leg muscles. "Hey, honey, you okay?"

"Sure." She set her first cut on the turntable and adjusted the needle.

"I caught the paper."

"No big deal, Bob."

"Hey, we're family around here." He gave her shoulder a quick squeeze. "We're behind you."

"Thanks."

"You're the cop?" he asked Boyd.

"That's right."

"Get this guy soon. He's got us all shaking." He gave Cilla another squeeze. "Let me know if you need anything."

"I will. Thanks."

She didn't want to think about it, couldn't afford to think about it, with thirty seconds to air. Taking her seat, she adjusted the mike, took a series of long, deep breaths, ran a one-two-three voice check, then opened her mike.

"All right, Denver, this is Cilla O'Roarke coming to you on number one, KHIP. You've got me from ten till two in the a.m. We're going to start off giving away one hundred and nine dollars. We've got the mystery record coming up. If you can give me the title, the artist and the year, you've got yourself a fistful of cash. That number is 555-5447. Stand by, 'cause we're going to rock.''

The music blasted out, pleasing her. She was in control again.

"Elton John," Boyd said from behind her. "'Honky Cat.' Nineteen seventy...two."

She turned in her chair to face him. He was looking damned pleased with himself, she thought. That half grin on his face, his hands in his pockets. It was a shame he was so attractive, a bloody crying shame. "Well, well, you surprise me, Slick. Remind me to put you down for a free T-shirt."

"I'd rather have a dinner."

"And I'd rather have a Porsche. But there you go— Hey," she said when he took her hand.

"You've been biting your nails." He skimmed a thumb over her knuckles and watched her eyes change. "Another bad habit."

"I've got lots more."

"Good." Instead of sitting back in the corner, he chose a chair beside her. "I didn't have time to get a book," he explained. "Why don't I watch you work?"

"Why don't you—" She swore, then punched a button on the phone. He'd nearly made her miss her cue. "KHIP. Can you name the mystery record?"

It took five calls before she had a winner. Trying to ignore Boyd, she put on another cut while she took the winner's name and address.

As if she didn't have enough on her mind, she thought. How was she supposed to concentrate on her show when he was all but sitting on top of her? Close enough, she realized, that she could smell him. No cologne, just soap—something that brought the mountains to mind one moment and quiet, intimate nights the next.

She wasn't interested in either, she reminded herself. All she wanted was to get through this crisis and get her life back on an even keel. Attractive men came and went, she knew. But success stayed—as long as you were willing to sweat for it.

She shifted, stretching out to select a new record. Their thighs brushed. His were long and as hard as rock. Determined not to jolt, she turned her head to look into his eyes. Inches apart, challenge meeting challenge. She watched as his gaze dipped down to linger on her mouth. And it lifted again, desire flickering. Music pulsed in her ears from the headphones she stubbornly wore so that she wouldn't have to speak to him. They were singing of hot nights and grinding needs.

Very carefully, she moved away. When she spoke into the mike again, her voice was even huskier.

He rose. He'd decided it was his only defense. He'd meant to annoy her, to distract her from the inevitable phone call that would come before the night was over. He'd wanted her mind off it, and on him. He wouldn't deny that he'd wanted her to think of him. But he hadn't known that when he'd succeeded she would tie him up in knots.

She smelled like midnight. Secret and sinful. She sounded like sex. Hot and inviting. Then you looked into her eyes, really looked, and saw simple innocence.

The man that combination wouldn't drive mad either had never been born or was already dead.

A little distance, Boyd told himself as he moved quietly out of the studio. A lot of objectivity. It wouldn't do either one of them any good to allow his emotions to get so tangled up with a woman he was supposed to protect.

When she was alone, Cilla made a conscious effort to relax, muscle by muscle. It was just because she was already on edge. It was a comfort to believe that. Her reaction to Boyd was merely an echo of the tension she'd lived with for more than a week. And he was trying to goad her.

She blew the hair out of her eyes and gave her listeners a treat—two hits in a row. And herself another moment to calm.

She hadn't figured him out yet. He read Steinbeck and recognized Elton John. He talked slow and lazy—and thought fast. He wore scarred boots and three-hundred-dollar jackets.

What did it matter? she asked herself as she set up for the next twenty minutes of her show. She wasn't interested in men. And he was definitely a man. Strike one. She would never consider getting involved with a cop. Strike two. And anyone with eyes could see that he had a close, even intimate relationship with his knockout partner. She'd never been one to poach on someone else's property.

Three strikes and he's out.

She closed her eyes and let the music pour through her. It helped, as it always did, to calm her, or lift her up, or simply remind her how lucky she was. She wasn't sharp and studious like Deborah. She wasn't dedicated, as their parents had been. She had little more than the education required by law, and yet she was here, just where she wanted to be, doing just what she wanted to do.

Life had taught her one vital lesson. Nothing lasted forever. Good times or bad, they passed. This nightmare, however horrid it was at this point in time, would be over eventually. She only had to get through it, one day at a time.

"That was Joan Jett waking you up as we head toward eleven-thirty. We've got a news brief coming up for you, then a double shot of Steve Winwood and Phil Collins to take us into the next half hour. This is KHIP, and the news is brought to you by Wildwood Records."

She punched in the prerecorded cassette, then scanned the printout of the ads and promos she would read. By the time Boyd came back, she was into the next block of music and standing up to stretch her muscles.

He stopped where he was, trying not to groan as she lifted her arms to the ceiling and rotated her hips. In time to the music, he was sure, as she bent from the waist, grabbed her ankles and slowly bent and straightened her knees.

He'd seen the routine before. It was something she did once or twice during her four-hour stint. But she thought she was alone now, and she put a little more rhythm into it. Watching her, he realized that the ten-minute break he'd taken hadn't been nearly long enough.

She sat again, pattered a bit to the audience. Her headphones were around her neck now, as she'd turned the music up for her own pleasure. As it pulsed, she swayed.

When he put a hand on her shoulder, she bolted out of the chair. "Easy, O'Roarke. I brought you some tea."

Her heart was like a trip-hammer in her chest. As it slowed, she lowered to the table. "What?"

"Tea," he repeated, offering her a cup. "I brought you some tea. You drink too much coffee. This is herbal. Jasmine or something."

She'd recovered enough to look at the cup in distaste. "I don't drink flowers."

"Try it. You might not hit the ceiling the next time someone touches you." He sipped a soft drink out of the bottle.

"I'd rather have that."

He took another sip, a long one, then passed the bottle to her. "You're almost halfway there."

Like Boyd, she looked at the clock. It was nearing midnight. This had once been her favorite leg of the show. Now, as she watched the second hand tick away, her palms began to sweat.

"Maybe he won't call tonight, since he got me at home."

He settled beside her again. "Maybe."

"But you don't think so."

"I think we take it a step at a time." He put a soothing hand at the back of her neck. "I want you to try to keep calm, keep him on the line longer. Ask questions. No matter what he says, just keep asking them, over and over. He may just answer one and give us something."

She nodded, then worked her way through the next ten minutes. "There's a question I want to ask you," she said at length.

"All right."

She didn't look at him, but drained the last swallow of the cold drink to ease her dry throat. "How long will they let me have a baby-sitter?"

"You don't have to worry about it."

"Let's just say I know something about how police departments work." It was there in her voice again, that touch of bitterness and regret. "A few nasty calls don't warrant a hell of a lot of attention."

"You're life's been threatened," he said. "It helps that you're a celebrity, and that there's already been some press on it. I'll be around for a while."

"Mixed blessings," she muttered, then opened the request line.

The call came, as she had known it would, but quickly this time. On call number five, she recognized the voice, battled back the urge to scream and switched to music. Without realizing it, she groped for Boyd's hand.

"You're persistent, aren't you?"

"I want you dead. I'm almost ready now."

"Do I know you? I like to think I know everyone who wants to kill me."

She winced a little at the names he spewed at her and tried to concentrate on the steady pressure of Boyd's fingers at the base of her neck.

"Wow. I've really got you ticked off. You know, buddy, if you don't like the show, you've just got to turn it off."

"You seduced him." There was a sound of weeping now, fueled with fury. "You seduced him, tempted him, promised him. Then you murdered him."

"I . . ." She was more shocked by this than by any of the gutter names he had called her. "Who? I don't know what you're talking about. Please, who—"

The line went dead.

As she sat there, dazed and silent, Boyd snatched up the phone. "Any luck? Damn it." He rose, stuffed his hands in his pockets and began pacing. "Another ten seconds. We'd have had him in another ten seconds. He has to know we've got it tapped." His head snapped around when Nick Peters entered, his hands full of sloshing coffee. "What?"

"I—I—I—" His Adam's apple bobbed as he swallowed. "Mark said it was okay if I stayed through the show." He swallowed again. "I thought Cilla might want some coffee."

Boyd jerked a thumb toward the table. "We'll let you know. Can you help her get through the rest of the show?"

"I don't need help." Cilla's voice was icy-calm. "I'm fine, Nick. Don't worry about it." She put a steady hand on the mike. "That was for Chuck from Laurie, with all her love." She aimed a steady look at Boyd before she punched the phone again. "KHIP, you're on the air."

She got through it. That was all that mattered. And she wasn't going to fall apart the way she had the other night. Cilla was grateful for that. All she needed to do was think it all through.

She hadn't objected when Boyd took the wheel of her car. Relinquishing the right to drive was the least of her worries.

"I'm coming in," Boyd said after he parked the car. She just shrugged and started for the door.

Very deliberately she hung up her coat and pried off her shoes. She sat, still without speaking, and lit a cigarette. The marked cruiser outside had relieved her mind. Deborah was safe and asleep.

"Look," she began once she'd marshaled her thoughts. "There really isn't any use going into this. I think I have it figured out."

"Do you?" He didn't sit down. Her icy calm disturbed him much more than hysterics or anger would have. "Fill me in."

"It's obvious he's made a mistake. He has me mixed up with someone else. I just have to convince him."

"Just have to convince him," Boyd repeated. "And how do you intend to do that?"

"The next time he calls, I'll make him listen." She crossed an arm across her body and began to rub at the chill in her shoulder. "For God's sake, Fletcher, I haven't murdered anyone."

"So you'll tell him that and he'll be perfectly reasonable and apologize for bothering you."

Her carefully built calm was wearing thin. "I'll make him understand."

"You're trying to make yourself believe he's rational, Cilla. He's not."

"What am I supposed to do?" she demanded, snapping the cigarette in two as she crushed it out. "Whether he's rational or not, I have to make him see he's made a mistake. I've never killed anyone." Her laugh was strained as she pulled the band from her hair. "I've never seduced anyone."

"Give me a break."

Anger brought her out of the chair. "What do you see me as, some kind of black widow who goes around luring men, then knocking them off when I'm finished? Get the picture, Fletcher. I'm a voice, a damn good one. That's where it ends."

"You're a great deal more than voice, Cilla. We both know that." He paused, waiting for her to look at him again. "And so does he."

Something trembled inside her—part fear, part longing. She wanted neither. "Whatever I am, I'm no temptress. It's an act, a show, and it has nothing to do with reality. My ex-husband would be the first to tell you I don't even have a sex drive."

His eyes sharpened. "You never mentioned you'd been married."

And she hadn't intended to, Cilla thought as she wearily combed a hand through her hair. "It was a million years ago. What does it matter?"

"Everything applies. I want his name and address."

"I don't know his address. We didn't even last a year. I was twenty years old, for God's sake." She began to rub at her forehead.

"His name, Cilla."

"Paul. Paul Lomax. I haven't seen him for about eight years—since he divorced me." She spun to the window, then back again. "The point is, this guy's on the wrong frequency. He's got it into his head I— what?—used my wiles on some guy, and that doesn't wash."

"Apparently he thinks it does."

"Well, he thinks wrong. I couldn't even keep one man happy, so it's a joke to think I could seduce legions."

"That's a stupid remark, even for you."

"Do you think I like admitting that I'm all show, that I'm lousy in bed?" She bit off the words as she paced. "The last man I went out with told me I had ice water for blood. But I didn't kill him." She calmed a little, amused in spite of herself. "I thought about it, though."

"I think it's time you start to take this whole business seriously. And I think it's time you start taking yourself seriously."

"I take myself very seriously."

"Professionally," he agreed. "You know exactly what to do and how to do it. Personally...you're the first woman I've met who was so willing to concede she couldn't make a man dance to her tune."

"I'm a realist."

"I think you're a coward."

Her chin shot up. "Go to hell."

He wasn't about to back off. He had a point to prove, to both of them. "I think you're afraid to get close to a man, afraid to find out just what's inside. Maybe you'd find out it's something you can't control."

"I don't need this from you. You just get this man off my back." She started to storm past him but was brought up short when he grabbed her arm.

"What do you say to an experiment?"

"An experiment?"

"Why don't you give it a try, O'Roarke—with me? It should be safe, since you can barely stand the sight of me. A test." He took her other arm. "Low-risk." He could feel the anger vibrate through her as he held her. Good. For reasons he couldn't have begun to name, he was just as angry. "Five to one I don't feel a thing." He drew her inches closer. "Want to prove me wrong?"

## Chapter 4

They were close. She had lifted one hand in an unconscious defensive gesture and now her fingers were splayed across his chest. She could feel his heartbeat, slow and steady, beneath her palm. She focused her resentment on that even rhythm as her own pulse jerked and scrambled.

"I don't have to prove anything to you."

He nodded. The barely banked fury in her eyes was easier for him to handle than the glaze of fear it replaced. "To yourself, then." Deliberately he smiled, baiting her. "What's the matter, O'Roarke? Do I scare you?"

He'd pushed exactly the right button. They both knew it. He didn't give a damn if it was temper that pushed her forward. As long as she moved.

She tossed her hair back and slowly, purposefully slid her hand from his chest to his shoulder. She wanted a reaction, hang him. He only lifted a brow and, with that faint smile playing around his mouth, watched her.

So he wanted to play games, she thought. Well, she was up for it. Tossing common sense aside, she pressed her lips to his.

His were firm, cool. And unresponsive. With her eyes open, she watched his remain patient, steady, and hatefully amused. As her hand balled into a fist on his shoulder, she snapped her head back.

"Satisfied?"

"Not hardly." His eyes might have been calm. That was training. But if she had bothered to monitor his heartbeat she would have found it erratic. "You're not trying, O'Roarke." He slid a hand down to her hip, shifting her balance just enough to have her sway against him. "You want me to believe that's the best you can do?"

Angry humiliation rippled through her. Cursing him, she dragged his mouth to hers and poured herself into the kiss.

His lips were still firm, but they were no longer cool. Nor were they unresponsive. For an instant the urge to retreat hammered at her. And then needs, almost forgotten needs, surged. A flood of longings, a storm of desires. Overwhelmed by them, she strained against him, letting the power and the heat whip through her, reminding her what it was like to sample passion again.

Every other thought, every other wish, winked out. She could feel the long, hard length of him pressed against her, the slow, deliberate stroke of his hands as they moved up her back and into her hair. His mouth, no longer patient, took and took from hers until the blood pounded like thunder in her head.

He'd known she would pack a punch. He'd thought he was prepared for it. In the days he'd known her he'd imagined tasting her like this dozens of times. He'd imagined what it would be like to hold her against him, to hear her sigh, to catch the fevered scent of her skin as he took his mouth over her.

But reality was much more potent than any dream had been.

Chain lightning. She was every bit as explosive, as turbulent, as potentially lethal. The current sparked and sizzled from her into him, leaving him breathless, dazed and churning. Even as he groaned against the onslaught, he felt her arch away from the power that snapped back into her.

She shuddered against him and made a sound—part protest, part confusion—as she tried to struggle away.

He'd wrapped her hair around his hand. He had only to tug gently to have her head fall back, to have her eyes dark and cloudy on his.

He took his time, letting his gaze skim over her face. He wanted to see in her eyes what he had felt. The reflection was there, that most elemental yearning. He smiled again as her lips trembled open and her breath came fast and uneven.

"I'm not finished yet," he told her, then dragged her against him again and plundered.

She needed to think, but her thoughts couldn't fight their way through the sensations. Layers of them, thin and silky, seemed to cover her, fogging the reason, drugging the will. Before panic could slice through, she was rocketing up again, clinging to him, opening for him, demanding from him.

He knew he could feast and never be full. Not when her mouth was hot and moist and ripe with flavor. He knew he could hold yet never control. Not when her body was vibrating from the explosion they had ignited together. The promise he had heard in her voice, seen in her eyes, was here for the taking.

Unable to resist, he slid his hands under her sweat-shirt to find the warmed satin skin beneath. He took, possessed, exploited, until the ache spreading through his body turned to pain.

Too fast, he warned himself. Too soon. For both of them. Holding her steady, he lifted his head and waited for her to surface.

She dragged her eyes open and saw only his face. She gulped in air and tasted only his flavor. Reeling, she pressed a hand to her temple, then let it fall to her side. "I . . . I want to sit down."

"That makes two of us." Taking her arm, he led her to the couch and sat beside her.

She worked on steadying her breathing, focused on the dark window across the room. Maybe with enough time, enough distance, she would be able to convince herself that what had just happened had not been life-altering.

"That was stupid."

"It was a lot of things," he pointed out. "Stupid doesn't come to mind."

She took one more deep breath. "You made me angry."

"It isn't hard."

"Listen, Boyd—"

"So you *can* say it." Before she could stop him, he stroked a hand down her hair in a casually intimate gesture that made her pulse rate soar again. "Does that mean you don't use a man's name until you've kissed him?"

"It doesn't mean anything." She stood up, hoping she'd get the strength back in her legs quicker by pacing. "Obviously we've gotten off the track."

"There's more than one." He settled back, thinking it was a pleasure to watch her move. There was something just fine and dandy about watching the swing of long feminine legs. As she paced, nervous energy crackling, he tossed an arm over the back of the couch and stretched out his legs.

"There's only one for me." She threw him a look over her shoulder. "You'd better understand that."

"Okay, we'll ride on that one for a while." He could afford to wait, since he had every intention of switching lines again, and soon. "You seem to have some kind of screwy notion that the only thing that attracts men to you is your voice, your act. I think we just proved you wrong."

"What just happened proved nothing." If there was anything more infuriating than that slow, patient smile of his, she had yet to see it. "In any case, that has nothing to do with the man who's calling me."

"You're a smart woman, Cilla. Use your head. He's fixed on you, but not for himself. He wants to pay you back for something you did to another man. Someone you knew," he continued when she stopped long enough to pick up a cigarette. "Someone who was involved with you."

"I've already told you, there's no one."

"No one now."

"No one now, no one before, no one for years."

Having experienced that first wave of her passion, he found that more than difficult to believe. Still, he nodded. "So it didn't mean as much to you. Maybe that's the problem."

"For God's sake, Fletcher, I don't even date. I don't have the time or the inclination."

"We'll talk about your inclinations later."

Weary, she turned away to stare blindly through the glass. "Damn it, Boyd, get out of my life."

"It's your life we're talking about." There was an edge to his voice that had her holding back the snide comment she wanted to make. "If there's been no one in Denver, we'll start working our way back. But I want you to think, and think hard. Who's shown an interest in you? Someone who calls the station more than normal. Who asks to meet you, asks personal questions. Someone who's approached you, asked you out, made a play."

She gave a short, humorless laugh. "You have."

"Remind me to run a make on myself." His voice was deceptively mild, but she caught the underlying annoyance and frustration in it. "Who else, Cilla?"

"There's no one, no one who's pushed." Wishing for a moment's, just a moment's, peace of mind, she pressed the heels of her hands against her eyes. "I get calls. That's the idea. I get some that ask me for a date, some that even send presents. You know, candy-and-flower types. Nothing very sinister about a bunch of roses."

"There's a lot sinister about death threats."

She wanted to speak calmly, practically, but she couldn't keep the nastiness out of her voice. "I can't remember everyone who's called and flirted with me on the air. Guys I turn down stay turned down."

He could only shake his head. It was a wonder to him that such a sharp woman could be so naive in certain situations. "All right, we'll shoot for a different angle. You work with men—almost all men—at the station."

"We're professionals," she snapped, and began biting her nails. "Mark's happily married. Bob's happily divorced. Jim's a friend—a good one."

"You forgot Nick."

"Nick Peters? What about him?"

"He's crazy about you."

"What?" She was surprised enough to turn around. "That's ridiculous. He's a kid."

After a long study, he let out a sigh. "You really haven't noticed, have you?"

"There's nothing to notice." More disturbed than she wanted to admit, she turned away again. "Look, Slick, this is getting us nowhere, and I'm . . ." Her words trailed off, and her hand crept slowly toward her throat.

"And you're what?"

"There's a man across the street. He's watching the house."

"Get away from the window."

"What?"

Boyd was already up and jerking her aside. "Stay away from the windows and keep the door locked. Don't open it again until I get back."

She nodded and followed him to the door. Her lips pressed together as she watched him take out his weapon. That single gesture snapped her back to reality. It had been a smooth movement, not so much practiced as instinctive. Ten years on the force, she remembered. He'd drawn and fired before.

She wouldn't tell him to be careful. Those were useless words.

"I'm going to take a look. Lock the door behind me." Gone was the laid-back man who had taunted her into an embrace. One look at his face and she could see that he was all cop. Their eyes changed, she thought. The emotion drained out of them. There was no room for emotion when you held a gun. "If I'm not back in ten minutes, call 911 for backup. Understood?"

"Yes." She gave in to the need to touch his arm. "Yes," she repeated.

After he slipped out, she shoved the bolt into place and waited.

He hadn't buttoned his coat, and the deep wind of the early hours whipped through his shirt. His weapon, warmed from sitting in its nest against his side, fitted snug in his hand. Sweeping his gaze right, then left, he found the street deserted, dark but for the pools of light from the streetlamps spaced at regular intervals. It was only a quiet suburban neighborhood, cozily asleep in the predawn hours. The night wind sounded through the naked trees in low moans.

He didn't doubt Cilla's words—wouldn't have doubted it even if he hadn't caught a glimpse through her window of a lone figure on the opposite sidewalk.

Whoever had been there was gone now, probably alerted the moment Cilla had spotted him.

As if to punctuate Boyd's thoughts, there was the sound of an engine turning over a block or two away. He swore but didn't bother to give chase. With that much of a lead, it would be a waste of time. Instead, he walked a half block in each direction, then carefully circled the house.

Cilla had her hand on the phone when he knocked.

"It's okay. It's Boyd."

In three hurried strides, she was at the door. "Did you see him?" she demanded the moment Boyd stepped inside.

"No."

"He was there. I swear it."

"I know." He relocked the door himself. "Try to relax. He's gone now."

"Relax?" In the past ten minutes she'd had more than enough time to work herself from upset to frantic. "He knows where I work, where I live. How in God's name am I ever supposed to relax again? If you hadn't scared him off, he might have—" She dragged her hands through her hair. She didn't want to think about what might have happened. Didn't dare.

Boyd didn't speak for a moment. Instead, he watched as she slowly, painfully brought herself under control. "Why don't you take some time off, stay home for a few days? We'll arrange for a black-and-white to cruise the neighborhood."

She allowed herself the luxury of sinking into a chair. "What difference does it make if I'm here or at the station?" She shook her head before he could speak. "And if I stayed home I'd go crazy thinking about it, worrying about it. At least at work I have other things on my mind."

He hadn't expected her to agree. "We'll talk about it later. Right now you're tired. Why don't you go to bed? I'll sleep on the couch."

She wanted to be strong enough to tell him it wasn't necessary. She didn't need to be protected. But the wave of gratitude made her weak. "I'll get you a blanket."

It was almost dawn when he dragged himself home. He'd driven a long time—from one sleepy suburb to another, into an eerily quiet downtown. Covering his trail. The panic had stayed with him for the first hour, but he'd beaten it, made himself drive slowly, carefully. Being stopped by a roving patrol car could have ruined all of his plans.

Under the heavy muffler and cap he was wearing he was sweating. In the thin canvas tennis shoes his feet were like ice. But he was too accustomed to discomfort to notice.

He staggered into the bathroom, never turning on a light. With ease he avoided his early-warning devices. The thin wire stretched from the arm of the spindly chair to the arm of the faded couch. The tower of cans at the entrance to his bedroom. He had excellent night vision. It was something he'd always been proud of.

He showered in the dark, letting the water run cold over his tensed body. As he began to relax, he allowed himself to draw in the fragrance of soap—his favorite scent. He used a rough, long-handled brush to violently scrub every inch of his skin.

As he washed, the dark began to lessen with the first watery light of dawn.

Over his heart was an intricate tattoo of two knives, blades crossed in an X. With his fingers he caressed them. He remembered when it had still been new, when he had shown it to John. John had been so impressed, so fascinated.

The image came so clearly. John's dark, excited eyes. His voice—the way he spoke so quickly that the words tumbled into each other. Sometimes they had sat in the dark and talked for hours, making plans and promises. They were going to travel together, do great things together.

Then the world had interfered. Life had interfered. The woman had interfered.

Dripping, he stepped from the shower. The towel was exactly where he had placed it. No one came into this room, into any of his rooms, to disturb his carefully ordered space. Once he was dry, he pulled on faded pajamas. They reminded him of the childhood he'd been cheated out of.

As the sun came up, he made two enormous sandwiches and ate them standing in the kitchen, leaning over the sink so that the crumbs wouldn't fall to the floor.

He felt strong again. Clean and fed. He was outwitting the police, making fools of them. And that delighted him. He was frightening the woman, bringing terror into every day of her life. That excited him. When the time was right, he would do everything he'd told her he would do.

And still it wouldn't be enough.

He went into the bedroom, shut the door, pulled the shades and picked up the phone.

Deborah strolled out of her room in a white teddy, a thin blue robe that reached to midthigh, flapping open. Her toenails were shocking pink. She'd painted them the night before to amuse herself as she'd crammed for an exam.

She was muttering the questions she thought would be on the exam she had scheduled at nine. The questions came easily enough, but the answers continued to bog down at some crossroads between the conscious and the unconscious. She hoped to unblock the answers with a quick shot of coffee.

Yawning, she stumbled over a boot, pitched toward the couch, then let out a muffled scream as her hand encountered warm flesh.

Boyd sat up like a shot, his hand already reaching for his weapon. With their faces close, he stared at Deborah—the creamy skin, the big blue eyes, the tumble of dark hair—and relaxed.

"Good morning."

"I—Detective Fletcher?"

He rubbed a hand over his eyes. "I think so."

"I'm sorry. I didn't realize you were here." She cleared her throat and belatedly remembered to close her robe. Still fumbling, she glanced up the stairs and automatically lowered her voice. Her sister wasn't a sound sleeper under the best of circumstances. "Why are you here?"

He flexed a shoulder that had stiffened during his cramped night on the couch. "I told you I was going to look after Cilla."

"Yes, you did." Her eyes narrowed as she studied him. "You take your job seriously."

"That's right."

"Good." Satisfied, she smiled. In the upheaval and confusion of her nineteen years, she had learned to make character judgments quickly. "I was about to make some coffee. I have an early class. Can I get you some?"

If she was anything like her sister, he wouldn't get any more sleep until he'd answered whatever questions were rolling around in her head. "Sure. Thanks."

"I imagine you'd like a hot shower, as well. You're about six inches too long to have spent a comfortable night on that couch."

"Eight," he said, rubbing the back of his stiff neck. "I think it's more like eight."

"You're welcome to all the hot water you want. I'll start on the coffee." As she turned toward the kitchen, the phone rang. Though she knew Cilla would pick it up before the second ring, she stepped toward it automatically. Boyd shook his head. Reaching over, he lifted the receiver and listened.

With her hands clutching the lapels of her robe, Deborah watched him. His face remained impassive, but she saw a flicker of anger in his eyes. Though brief, it was intense enough to make her certain who was on the other end of the line.

Boyd disconnected mechanically, then punched in a series of numbers. "Anything?" He didn't even bother to swear at the negative reply. "Right." After hanging up, he looked at Deborah. She was standing beside the couch, her hands clenched, her face pale. "I'm going upstairs," he said. "I'll take a rain check on that coffee."

"She'll be upset. I want to talk to her."

He pushed aside the blanket and rose, wearing only his jeans. "I'd appreciate it if you'd let me handle it this time."

She wanted to argue, but something in his eyes stopped her. She nodded. "All right, but do a good job of it. She isn't as tough as she likes people to think."

"I know."

He climbed the stairs to the second floor, walked past an open door to a room where the bed was tidily made. Deborah's, he decided, noting the rose-and-white decor and the feminine bits of lace. Pausing at the next door, he knocked, then entered without waiting for an answer.

She was sitting in the middle of the bed, her knees drawn up close to her chest and her head resting on them. The sheets and blankets were tangled, a testimony to the few hours of restless sleep she'd had.

There were no bits of feminine lace here, no soft, creamy colors. She preferred clean lines rather than curves, simplicity rather than flounces. In contrast, the color scheme was electric, and anything but restful. In the midst of the vibrant blues and greens, she seemed all the more vulnerable.

She didn't look up until he sat on the edge of the bed and touched her hair. Slowly she lifted her head. He saw that there were no tears. Rather than the fear he'd expected, there was an unbearable weariness that was even more disturbing.

"He called," she said.

"I know. I was on the extension."

"Then you heard." She looked away, toward the window, where she could see the sun struggling to burn away a low bank of clouds. "It was him outside last night. He said he'd seen me, seen us. He made it sound revolting."

"Cilla—"

"He was watching!" She spit out the words. "Nothing I say, nothing I do, is going to make him stop. And if he gets to me, he's going to do everything he said he'd do.''

"He's not going to get to you.''

"How long?'' she demanded. Her fingers clenched and unclenched on the sheets as her eyes burned into his. "How long can you watch me? He'll just wait. He'll wait and keep calling, keep watching.'' Something snapped inside her, and she picked up the bedside phone and heaved it across the room. It bounced against the wall, jangling as it thudded to the floor. "You're not going to stop him. You heard him. He said nothing would stop him.''

"This is just what he wants.'' Boyd took her by the arms and gave her one quick shake. "He wants you to fall apart. He wants to know he's made you fall apart. If you do, you're only helping him.''

"I don't know what to do,'' she managed. "I just don't know what to do.''

"You've got to trust me. Look at me, Cilla.'' Her breath was hitching, but she met his eyes. "I want you to trust me,'' he said quietly, "and believe me when I say I won't let anything happen to you.''

"You can't always be there.''

His lips curved a little. He gentled his hold to rub his hands up and down her arms. "Sure I can.''

"I want—'' She squeezed her eyes shut. How she hated to ask. Hated to need.

"What?''

Her lips trembled as she fought for one last hand-hold on control. "I need to hold on to something.'' She let out an unsteady breath. "Please.''

He said nothing, but he gathered her close to cradle her head on his shoulder. Her hands, balled into fists, pressed against his back. She was trembling, fighting off a wild bout of tears.

"Take five, O'Roarke," he murmured. "Let loose."

"I can't." She kept her eyes closed and held on. He was solid, warm, strong. Dependable. "I'm afraid once I do I won't be able to stop."

"Okay, let's try this." He tilted her head up and touched his lips gently to hers. "Think about me. Right here." His mouth brushed hers again. "Right now." Easy, patient, he stroked her rigid back. "Just me."

Here was compassion. She hadn't known a kiss from a man could hold it. More than gentle, more than tender, it soothed frayed nerves, calmed icy fears, cooled hot despair. Her clenched hands relaxed, muscle by muscle. There was no demand here as his lips roamed over her face. Just understanding.

It became so simple to do as he'd asked. She thought only of him.

Hesitant, she brought a hand to his face, letting her fingers skim along his beard-roughened cheek. Her stomach unknotted. The throbbing in her head quieted. She said his name on a sigh and melted against him.

He had to be careful. Very careful. Her complete and total surrender had his own needs drumming. He ignored them. For now she needed comfort, not passion. It couldn't matter that his senses were reeling from her, the soft give of her body, the rich taste of her mouth. It couldn't matter that the air had thickened so that each breath he took was crowded with the scent of her.

He knew he had only to lay her back on the bed among the tangled sheets. And cover her. She wouldn't resist. Perhaps she would even welcome the heat and the distraction. The temporary respite. He intended to be much more to her.

Battling his own demons, he pressed his lips to her forehead, then rested his cheek on her hair.

"Better?"

On one ragged breath, she nodded. She wasn't sure she could speak. How could she tell him that she wanted only to stay like this, her arms around him, his heart beating against hers? He'd think she was a fool.

"I, uh...didn't know you could be such a nice guy, Fletcher."

He wanted to sigh, but he found himself grinning. "I have my moments."

"Yeah. Well, that was certainly above and beyond."

Maybe, just maybe, she wasn't really trying to needle him. He pulled back, put a hand under her chin and held it steady. "I'm not on duty. When I kiss you, it's got nothing to do with my job. Got it?"

She'd meant to thank him, not annoy him. There was a warning in his eyes that had her frowning. "Sure."

"Sure," he repeated, then rose to jam his hands in his pockets in disgust.

For the first time she noted that he wore only his jeans, unsnapped and riding low. The sudden clutching in her stomach had nothing to do with fear and left her momentarily speechless.

She wanted him. Not just to hold, not just for a few heated kisses. And certainly not just for comfort. She wanted him in bed, the way she couldn't remember ever wanting a man before. She could look at him—the long, lean, golden line of torso, the narrow hips, the dance of muscle in his arms as he balled his hands—and she could imagine what it would be like to touch and be touched, to roll over the bed in one tangled heap of passion. To ride and be ridden.

"What the hell's wrong with you now?"

"What?"

Eyes narrowed, he rocked back on his heels as she blinked at him. "Taking a side trip, O'Roarke?"

"I, ah . . ." Her mouth was dry, and there was a hard knot of pressure in her gut. What would he say if she told him where her mind had just taken her, taken them? She let her eyes close. "Oh, boy," she whispered. "I think I need some coffee." And a quick dip in a cold lake.

"Your sister was fixing some." He frowned as he studied her. He thought of Deborah for a moment, of how she had nearly fallen on top of him wearing hardly more than a swatch of white lace. He'd appreciated the long, lissome limbs. What man wouldn't? But looking at her hadn't rocked his system.

And here was Cilla—sitting there with her eyes shadowed, wearing a Broncos football jersey that was two sizes too big. The bright orange cotton was hardly seductive lingerie. If he stood there one more moment, he would be on his knees begging for mercy.

"How about breakfast?" His voice was abrupt, not even marginally friendly. It helped to bring her thoughts to order.

"I never eat it."

"Today you do. Ten minutes."

"Look, Slick—"

"Do something with your hair," he said as he walked out of the room. "You look like hell."

He found Deborah downstairs in the kitchen, fully dressed, sipping a cup of coffee. That she was waiting for him was obvious. The moment he stepped into the room she was out of her chair.

"She's fine," he said briefly. "I'm going to fix her some breakfast."

Though her brow lifted at this information, she nodded. "Look, why don't you sit down? I'll fix some for both of you."

"I thought you had an early class."

"I'll skip it."

He headed for the coffee. "Then she'll be mad at both of us."

She had to smile as he poured a cup, then rooted through a drawer for a spoon for the sugar. "You already know her very well."

"Not well enough." He drank half the cup and felt nearly human again. He had to think of Cilla. It would be safe enough, he hoped, if he kept those thoughts professional. "How much time do you have?"

"About five minutes," she said as she glanced at her watch.

"Tell me about the ex-husband."

"Paul?" There was surprise in her eyes, in her voice. "Why?" She was shaking her head before he could answer. "You don't think he has anything to do with what's going on here?"

"I'm checking all the angles. The divorce...was it amicable?"

"Are they ever?"

She was young, Boyd thought, nodding, but she was sharp. "You tell me."

"Well, in this case, I'd say it was as amicable—or as bland as they get." She hesitated, torn. If it was a question of being loyal to Cilla or protecting her, she had to choose protection. "I was only about twelve, and Cilla was never very open about it, but my impression was, always has been, that he wanted it."

Boyd leaned back against the counter. "Why?"

Uncomfortable, Deborah moved her shoulders. "He'd fallen in love with someone else." She let out a hiss of breath and prayed Cilla wouldn't see what she was doing as a betrayal. "It was pretty clear that they were having problems before I came to live with them. It was right after our parents had died. Cilla had only been married a few months, but . . . well, let's say the honeymoon was over. She was making a name for herself in Atlanta, and Paul—he was very conservative, a real straight arrow. He'd decided to run for assemblyman, I think it was, and Cilla's image didn't suit."

"Sounds like it was the other way around to me."

She smiled then, beautifully, and moved over to top off his coffee. "I remember how hard she was working, to hold her job together, to hold everything together. It was a pretty awful time for us. It didn't help matters when the responsibility for a twelve-year-old was suddenly dumped on them. The added strain—well, I guess you could say it hastened the inevitable. A couple of months after I moved in, he moved out and filed for divorce. She didn't fight it."

He tried to imagine how it would have been. At twenty, she'd lost her parents, accepted the care and responsibility of a young girl and watched her marriage crumble. "Sounds to me like she was well rid of him."

"I guess it doesn't hurt to say I never liked him very much. He was inoffensive. And dull."

"Why did she marry him?"

"I think it would be more appropriate to ask me," Cilla said from the doorway.

## Chapter 5

The something she had done with her hair was to pull it back in a ponytail. It left her face unframed, so the anger in her eyes was that much easier to read. Along with the jersey she'd slept in, she'd pulled on a pair of yellow sweatpants. It was a deceptively sunny combination. Her hands were thrust into their deep pockets as she stood, directing all her resentment at Boyd.

"Cilla." Knowing there was a time to argue and a time to soothe, Deborah stepped forward. "We were just—"

"Yes, I heard what you were just." She shifted her gaze to Deborah. The edge of her temper softened. "Don't worry about it. It's not your fault."

"It's not a matter of fault," Deborah murmured. "We care what happens to you."

"Nothing's going to happen. You'd better get going, Deb, or you'll be late. And it appears that Detective Fletcher and I have things to discuss."

Deborah lifted her hands and let them fall. She shot one sympathetic glance toward Boyd, then kissed her sister's cheek. "All right. You'd never listen to reason at this hour anyway."

"Get an A," was all Cilla said.

"I intend to. I'm going to catch a burger and a movie with Josh, but I'll be back before you get home."

"Have a good time." Cilla waited, not moving an inch until she heard the front door close. "You've got a hell of a nerve, Fletcher."

He merely turned and slipped another mug off the hook behind the stove. "Want some coffee?"

"I don't appreciate you grilling my sister."

He filled the mug, then set it aside. "I left my rubber hose in my other suit."

"Let's get something straight." She walked toward him, deliberately keeping her hands in her pockets. She was dead sure she'd hit him if she took them out. "If you have any questions about me, you come to me. Deborah is not involved in any of this."

"She's a lot more forthcoming than her sister. Got any eggs?" he asked as he opened the refrigerator.

She managed to restrain the urge to kick the door into his head. "You know, for a minute upstairs you had me fooled. I actually thought you had some heart, some compassion."

He found a half-dozen eggs, some cheese and a few miserly strips of bacon. "Why don't you sit down, O'Roarke, and drink your coffee?"

She swore at him, viciously. Something shot into his eyes, something dangerous, but he picked up a skillet and calmly began to fry the bacon. "You'll have to do better than that," he said after a moment. "After ten years on the force there's not much you could call me and get a rise."

"You had no right." Her voice had quieted, but the emotion in it had doubled. "No right to dredge all that up with her. She was a child, devastated, scared to death. That entire year was nothing but hell for her, and she doesn't need you to make her remember it."

"She handled herself just fine." He broke an egg into a bowl, then crushed the shell in his hand. "It seems to me you're the one with the problem."

"Just back off."

He had her arm in a tight grip so quickly that she had no chance to evade. His voice was soft, deadly, with temper licking around the edges. "Not a chance."

"What happened back then has nothing to do with what's happening now, and what's happening now is the only thing that concerns you."

"It's my job to determine what applies." With an effort, he reeled himself in. He couldn't remember when anyone had pushed him so close to the edge so often. "If you want me to put it to rest, then spell it out for me. Ex-spouses are favored suspects."

"It was eight years ago." She jerked away and, needing something to do with her hands, snatched up her coffee. It splattered over the rim and onto the counter.

"I find out from you or I find out from someone else. The end result's the same."

"You want me to spell it out? You want me to strip bare? Fine. It hardly matters at this point. I was twenty, I was stupid. He was beautiful and charming and smart—all the things stupid twenty-year-old girls think they want."

She took a long sip of hot coffee, then automatically reached for a washcloth to mop up the spill. "We only knew each other a couple of months. He was very persuasive, very romantic. I married him because I wanted something stable and real in my life. And I thought he loved me."

She was calmer now. She hadn't realized that the anger had drained away. Sighing, she turned, mechanically reaching for plates and flatware. "It didn't work—almost from day one. He was disappointed in me physically and disillusioned when he saw that I believed my work was as important as his. He'd hoped to convince me to change jobs. Not that he wanted me to quit altogether. He wasn't against my having a career, even in radio—as long as it didn't interfere with his plans."

"Which were?" Boyd asked as he set the bacon aside to drain.

"Politics. Actually, we met at a charity event the station put on. He was trying to charm up votes. I was promoting. That was the basic problem," she murmured. "We met each other's public personalities."

"What happened?"

"We got married—too fast. And things went wrong—too fast. I was even considering his idea that I go into marketing or sales. I figured I should at least give it a shot. Then my parents... I lost my parents, and brought Deborah home."

She stopped speaking for a moment. She couldn't talk of that time, couldn't even think of the fears and the griefs, the pain and the resentments.

"It must have been rough."

She shrugged the words away. "The bottom line was, I couldn't handle another upheaval. I needed to work. The strain ate away at what shaky foundation we had. He found someone who made him happier, and he left me." She filled her mug with coffee she no longer wanted. "End of story."

What was he supposed to say? Boyd wondered. Tough break, kid? We all make mistakes? You were better off without the jerk? No personal comments, he warned himself. They were both edgy enough.

"Did he ever threaten you?"

"No."

"Abuse you?"

She gave a tired laugh. "No. No. You're trying to make him into the bad guy, Boyd, and it won't play. We were simply two people who made a mistake because we got married before we knew what we wanted."

Thoughtful, Boyd scooped eggs onto her plate. "Sometimes people hold resentments without even being aware of it. Then one day they bust loose."

"He didn't resent me." Sitting, she picked up a piece of bacon. She studied it as she broke it in two. "He never cared enough for that. That's the sad, sad truth." She smiled, but there wasn't a trace of humor in her eyes. "You see, he thought I was like the woman he heard on the radio—seductive, sophisticated, sexy. He wanted that kind of woman in bed. And outside the bedroom he wanted a well-groomed, well-mannered, attentive woman to make his home. I was neither." She shrugged and dropped the bacon on her plate again. "Since he wasn't the attentive, reliable and understanding man I thought he was, we both lost out. We had a very quiet, very civilized divorce, shook hands and went our separate ways."

"If there was nothing more to it, why are you still raw?"

She looked up then, eyes somber. "You've never been married, have you?"

"No."

"Then I couldn't begin to explain. If you want to run a check on Paul, you go ahead, but it's a waste of time. I can guarantee he hasn't given me a thought since I left Atlanta."

He doubted that any man who had ever been close to her would be able to push her completely out of his mind, but he would let that ride for the moment. "You're letting your eggs get cold."

"I told you I don't eat breakfast."

"Humor me." He reached over, scooped up a forkful of eggs from her plate and held them to her lips.

"You're a pest," she said after she swallowed them. "Don't you have to check in or something?"

"I already did—last night, after you went up to bed."

She toyed with the food on her plate, eating a bite or two to keep him from nagging her. He had stayed, she reminded herself, long after his duty shift was over. She owed him for that. And she always paid her debts.

"Look, I appreciate you hanging around, and I know it's your job to ask all kinds of personal and embarrassing questions. But I really want you to leave Deb out of it."

"As much as I can."

"Spring break's coming up. I'm going to try to convince her to head for the beach."

"Good luck." He sipped, watching her over the rim of his mug. "You might pull it off if you went with her."

"I'm not running from this." After pushing her half-eaten breakfast aside, she rested her elbows on the table. "After the call this morning, I was pretty close to doing just that. I thought about it—and after I did I realized it's not going to stop until I figure it out. I want my life back, and that's not going to happen until we know who he is and why he's after me."

"It's my job to find him."

"I know. That's why I've decided to cooperate."

He set his mug aside. "Have you?"

"That's right. From now on, my life's an open book. You ask, I'll answer."

"And you'll do exactly what you're told?"

"No." She smiled. "But I'll do exactly what I'm told if it seems reasonable." She surprised them both by reaching over to touch his hand. "You look tired, Slick. Rough night?"

"I've had better." He linked his fingers with hers before she could withdraw them. "You look damn good in the morning, Cilla."

There it was again—that fluttering that started in her chest and drifted down to her stomach. "A little while ago you said I looked like hell."

"I changed my mind. Before I clock in I'd like to talk to you about last night. About you and me."

"That's not a good idea."

"No, it's not." But he didn't release her hand. "I'm a cop, and you're my assignment. There's no getting around that." She nearly managed a relieved breath before he continued. "Any more than there's any getting around the fact that I want you so much it hurts."

She went very still, so still she could hear the sound of her own heartbeat drumming in her head. Very slowly she moved her eyes, only her eyes, until they met his. They were not so calm now, she thought. There was a fire there, barely banked. It was exciting, terrifyingly exciting.

"Lousy timing," he continued when she didn't speak. "But I figure you can't always pick the right time and the right place. I'm going to do my job, but I think you should know I'm having trouble being objective. If you want someone else assigned to you, you'd better say so now."

"No." She answered too quickly, and she forced herself to backtrack. "I don't think I'm up to breaking in a new cop." Keep it light, she warned herself. "I'm not crazy about having one at all, but I'm almost used to you." She caught herself gnawing on her thumbnail and hastily dropped her hand into her lap. "As for the rest, we're not children. We can . . . handle it."

He knew he shouldn't expect her to admit the wanting wasn't all one-sided. So he would wait a little while longer.

When he rose, she sprang up so quickly that he laughed. "I'm going to do the dishes, O'Roarke, not jump on you."

"I'll do them." She could have kicked herself. "One cooks, one cleans. O'Roarke rules."

"Fine. You've got a remote at noon, right?"

"How did you know?"

"I checked your schedule. Leave enough time for us to drop by my place so I can shower and change."

"I'm going to be in a mall with dozens of people," she began. "I don't think—"

"I do." With that, he left her alone.

Boyd was lounging on the couch with the paper and a last cup of coffee when Cilla came downstairs. He glanced over, and the casual comment he'd been about to make about her being quick to change died before it reached his tongue. He was glad he was sitting down.

She wore red. Vivid, traffic-stopping red. The short leather skirt was snug at the hips and stopped at mid-thigh. The jeans she usually wore hadn't given him a true measure of how long her legs were, or how shapely. The matching jacket crossed over her body to side snaps at the waist. It made him wonder what she was wearing beneath it.

She'd done something to her hair. It was still tumbled, but more artfully, and certainly more alluringly. And her face, he noted as he finally stood. She'd fiddled with that, as well—enough to highlight her cheekbones, accent her eyes, slicken her lips.

"Stupid," she muttered as she struggled with an earring. "I can never figure out why hanging things from your ears is supposed to be attractive." On a sigh, she stared down at the dangling columns and the little gold back in her palm. "Either these are defective or I am. Are you any good at this?"

She'd walked to him, her hand held out. Her scent was wheeling in his head. "At what?"

"Putting these in. I don't wear them for weeks at a time, so I've never really gotten the hang of it. Give me a hand, will you?"

He was concentrating on breathing, nice, slow, even breaths. "You want me to put that on for you?"

She rolled her eyes impatiently. "You catch on fast, Slick." She thrust the earring into his hand, then tucked the hair behind her right ear. "You just slide the post through, then fasten the little doodad on the back. That's the part I have trouble with."

He muttered something, then bent to the task. There was a pressure in his chest, and it was building. He knew he would never get that scent out of his system. Swearing softly, he struggled to pinch the tiny fastening with his fingertips.

"This is a stupid system."

"Yeah." She could barely speak. She'd known the minute he touched her that she'd made an enormous mistake. Bursts of sensations, flashes of images, were rushing into her. All she could do was stand still and pray he'd hurry up and finish.

The back of his thumb brushed up and down over her jaw. His fingertips grazed the sensitive area behind her ear. His breath fluttered warm against her skin until she had to bite back a moan.

She lifted an unsteady hand. "Listen, why don't we just forget it?"

"I've got it." Letting out a long breath, he stepped back an inch. He was a wreck. But some of the tension eased when he looked at her and saw that she was far from unaffected. He managed to smile then and flicked a finger over the swaying gold columns. "We'll have to try that again . . . when we've got more time."

Since no response she could think of seemed safe, she gave none. Instead, she retrieved his coat and her own from the closet. She set his aside and waited while he slipped into his shoulder holster. Watching him give his weapon a quick, routine check brought back memories she wanted to avoid, so she looked away. Pulling open the door, she stepped into the sunlight and left him to follow when he was ready.

He made no comment when he joined her.

"Do you mind if I tune the station in?" she asked as they settled into his car.

"It's on memory. Number three."

Pleased, she turned it on. The morning team was chattering away, punctuating their jokes with sound effects. They plugged an upcoming concert, promised to give another pair of tickets away during the next hour, then invited the listening audience to the mall to see Cilla O'Roarke live and in person.

"She'll be giving away albums, T-shirts and concert tickets," Frantic Fred announced.

"Come on, Fred," his partner broke in. "You know those guys out there don't care about a couple of T-shirts. They want to—" he made loud, panting noises— "see Cilla." There was a chorus of wolf whistles, growls and groans.

"Cute," Boyd muttered, but Cilla only chuckled.

"They're supposed to be obnoxious," she pointed out. "People like absurdity in the morning when they're dragging themselves out of bed or fighting traffic. Last quarter's Arbitron ratings showed them taking over twenty-four percent of the target audience."

"I guess you get a kick out of hearing some guy pant over you."

"Hey, I live for it." Too amused to be offended, she settled back. He certainly had a nice car for a cop. Some sporty foreign job that still smelled new. She was never any good with makes and models. "Come on, Slick, it's part of the act."

He caught himself before he could speak again. He was making a fool of himself. His own investigation had verified that both morning men were married, with tidy homes in the suburbs. Frantic Fred and his wife were expecting their first child. Both men had been with KHIP for nearly three years, and he'd found no cross-reference between their pasts and Cilla's.

Relaxing as the music began, Cilla gazed out the window. The day promised to be warm and sunny. Perhaps this would be the first hint of spring. And her first spring in Colorado. She had a weakness for the season, for watching the leaves bud and grow, the flowers bloom.

Yet in spring she would always think of Georgia. The magnolias, the camellias, the wisterias. All those heady scents.

She remembered a spring when she'd been five or six. Planting peonies with her father on a warm Saturday morning while the radio counted down the Top 40 hits of the week. Hearing the birds without really listening, feeling the damp earth under her hands. He'd told her they would bloom spring after spring and that she would be able to see them from her window.

She wondered if they were still there—if whoever lived in that house cared for them.

"Cilla?"

She snapped back. "What?"

"Are you all right?"

"Sure, I'm fine." She focused on her surroundings. There were big trees that would shade in the summer, trimmed hedges for privacy. A long, gently sloping hill led to a graceful three-story house fashioned from stone and wood. Dozens of tall, slender windows winked in the sunlight. "Where are we?"

"My house. I've got to change, remember?"

"Your house?" she repeated.

"Right. Everyone has to live somewhere."

True enough, she thought as she pushed the door open. But none of the cops she had ever known had lived so well. A long look around showed her that the neighborhood was old, established and wealthy. A country-club neighborhood.

Disconcerted, she followed Boyd up a stone path to an arched door outlined in etched glass.

Inside, the foyer was wide, the floors a gleaming cherry, the ceilings vaulted. On the walls were paintings by prominent twentieth-century artists. A sweep of stairway curved up to the second floor.

"Well," she said. "And I thought you were an honest cop."

"I am." He slipped the coat from her shoulders to toss it over the railing.

She had no doubts as to his honesty, but the house and all it represented made her nervous. "And I suppose you inherited all this from a rich uncle."

"Grandmother." Taking her arm, he led her through a towering arch. The living room was dominated by a stone fireplace topped with a heavy carved mantel. But the theme of the room was light, with a trio of windows set in each outside wall.

There was a scattering of antiques offset by modern sculpture. She could see what she thought was a dining room through another arch.

"That must have been some grandmother."

"She was something. She ran Fletcher Industries until she hit seventy."

"And what is Fletcher Industries?"

He shrugged. "Family business. Real estate, cattle, mining."

"Mining." She blew out a breath. "Like gold?"

"Among other things."

She linked her fingers together to keep from biting her nails. "So why aren't you counting your gold instead of being a cop?"

"I like being a cop." He took her restless hand in his. "Something wrong?"

"No. You'd better change. I have to be there early to prep."

"I won't be long."

She waited until he had gone before she sank onto one of the twin sofas. Fletcher Industries, she thought. It sounded important. Even prominent. After digging in her bag for a cigarette, she studied the room again.

Elegant, tasteful, easily rich. And way out of her league.

It had been difficult enough when she'd believed they were on fairly equal terms. She didn't like to admit it, but the thought had been there, in the back of her mind, that maybe, just maybe, there could be a relationship between them. No, a friendship. She could never be seriously involved with someone in law enforcement.

But he wasn't just a cop now. He was a rich cop. His name was probably listed on some social register. People who lived in houses like this usually had roman numerals after their names.

Boyd Fletcher III.

She was just Priscilla Alice O'Roarke, formerly from a backwater town in Georgia that wasn't even a smudge on the map. True, she had made something of herself, by herself. But you never really pulled out your roots.

Rising, she walked over to toss her cigarette in the fireplace.

She wished he would hurry. She wanted to get out of this house, get back to work. She wanted to forget about the mess her life was suddenly in.

She had to think about herself. Where she was going. How she was going to get through the long days and longer nights until her life was settled again. She didn't have the time, she couldn't afford the luxury of exploring her feelings for Boyd. Whatever she had felt, or thought she was feeling, was best ignored.

If ever there were two people more mismatched, she couldn't imagine them. Perhaps he had stirred something in her, touched something she'd thought could never be touched again. It meant nothing. It only proved that she was alive, still functioning as a human being. As a woman.

It would begin and end there.

The minute whoever was threatening her was caught, they would go their separate ways, back to their separate lives. Whatever closeness they had now was born of necessity. When the necessity passed, they would move apart and forget. Nothing, she reminded herself, lasted forever.

She was standing by the windows when he came back. The light was in her hair, on her face. He had never imagined her there, but somehow, when he looked, when he saw her, he knew he'd wanted her there.

It left him shaken, it left him aching to see how perfectly she fitted into his home. Into his life. Into his dreams.

She would argue about that, he thought. She would struggle and fight and run like hell if he gave her the chance. He smiled as he crossed to her. He just wouldn't give her the chance.

"Cilla."

Startled, she whirled around. "Oh. I didn't hear you. I was—"

The words were swallowed by a gasp as he yanked her against him and imprisoned her mouth.

Earthquakes, floods, wild winds. How could she have known that a kiss could be grouped with such devastating natural disasters?

She didn't want this. She wanted it more than she wanted to breathe. She had to push him away. She pulled him closer. It was wrong, it was madness. It was right, it was beautifully mad.

As she pressed against him, as her mouth answered each frenzied demand, she knew that everything she had tried to convince herself of only moments before was a lie. What need was there to explore her feelings when they were all swimming to the surface?

She needed him. However much that might terrify her, for now the knowledge and the acceptance flowed through her like wine. It seemed she had waited a lifetime to need like this. To feel like this. Trembling and strong, dazed and clear-eyed, pliant and taut as a wire.

His hands whispered over the leather as he molded her against him. Couldn't she see how perfectly they fitted? He wanted to hear her say it, to hear her moan it, that she wanted him as desperately as he wanted her.

She did moan as he drew her head back to let his lips race down her throat. The thudding of her pulse heated the fragrance she'd dabbed there. Groaning as it tangled in his senses, he dragged at the snaps of her jacket. Beneath he found nothing but Cilla.

She arched back, her breath catching in her throat as he captured her breasts. At his touch it seemed they filled with some hot, heavy liquid. When her knees buckled, she gripped his shoulders for balance, shuddering as his thumbs teased her nipples into hard, aching peaks.

Mindlessly she reached for him, diving into a deep, intimate kiss that had each of them swaying. She tugged at his jacket, desperate to touch him as he touched her. Her hand slid over the leather of his holster and found his weapon.

It was like a slap, like a splash of ice water. As if burned, she snatched her hand away and jerked back. Unsteady, she pressed the palm of her hand against a table and shook her head.

"This is a mistake." She paced her words slowly, as if she were drunk. "I don't want to get involved."

"Too late." He felt as if he'd slammed full tilt into a wall.

"No." With deliberate care, she snapped her jacket again. "It's not too late. I have a lot on my mind. So do you."

He struggled for the patience that had always been part of his nature. For the first time in days he actively craved a cigarette. "And?"

"And nothing. I think we should go."

He didn't move toward her or away, but simply held up a hand. "Before we do, are you going to tell me you don't feel anything?"

She made herself look at him. "It would be stupid to pretend I'm not attracted to you. You already know you affect me."

"I want to bring you back here tonight."

She shook her head. She couldn't afford, even for an instant, to imagine what it would be like to be with him. "I can't. There are reasons."

"You've already told me there isn't anyone else." He stepped toward her now, but he didn't touch her. "If there was, I wouldn't give a damn."

"This has nothing to do with other men. It has to do with me."

"Exactly. Why don't you tell me what you're afraid of?"

"I'm afraid of picking up the phone." It was true, but it wasn't the reason. "I'm afraid of going to sleep, and I'm afraid of waking up."

He touched her then, just a fingertip to her cheek. "I know what you're going through, and believe me, I'd do anything to make it go away. But we both know that's not the reason you're backing away from me."

"I have others."

"Give me one."

Annoyed, she walked over to grab her purse. "You're a cop."

"And?"

She tossed her head up. "So was my mother." Before he could speak, she was striding back into the foyer to get her coat.

"Cilla—"

"Just back off, Boyd. I mean it." She shoved her arms into her coat. "I can't afford to get churned up like this before a show. For God's sake, my life's screwed up enough right now without this. If you can't let it alone, I'll call your captain and tell him I want someone else assigned. Now you can take me to the mall or I can call a cab."

One more push and she'd be over the edge, he thought. This wasn't the time for her to take that tumble. "I'll take you," he said. "And I'll back off. For now."

## Chapter 6

He was a man of his word, Cilla decided. For the rest of that day, and all of the next, they discussed nothing that didn't relate directly to the case.

He wasn't distant. Far from it. He stuck with her throughout her remote at the mall, subtly screening all the fans who approached her for a word or an autograph, all the winners who accepted their T-shirts or their albums.

It even seemed to Cilla that he enjoyed himself. He browsed through the record racks, buying from the classical, pop and jazz sections, chatted with the engineer about baseball and kept her supplied with a steady supply of cold soft drinks in paper cups.

He talked, but she noted that he didn't talk *to* her, not the way she'd become accustomed to. They certainly had conversations, polite and impersonal conversations. And not once, not even in the most casual of ways, did he touch her.

In short, he treated her exactly the way she'd thought she wanted to be treated. As an assignment, and nothing more.

While he seemed to take the afternoon in stride, even offering to buy her a burger between the end of the remote and the time she was expected back in the studio, she was certain she'd never spent a more miserable afternoon in her life.

It was Althea who sat with her in the booth over her next two shifts, and it was Althea who monitored the calls. Why Boyd's silence, and his absence, made it that much more difficult for her to concentrate, Cilla couldn't have said.

It was probably some new strategy, she decided as she worked. He was ignoring her so that she would break down and make the first move. Well, she wouldn't. She hit her audience with Bob Seger's latest gritty rock single and stewed.

She'd wanted their relationship to be strictly professional, and he was accommodating her. But he didn't have to make it seem so damned easy.

Undoubtedly what had happened between them—or what had almost happened between them—hadn't really meant that much to him. That was all for the best. She would get over it. Whatever it was. The last thing she needed in her life was a cop with a lazy smile who came from a moneyed background.

She wished to God she could go five minutes without thinking about him.

While Cilla juggled turntables, Althea worked a crossword puzzle. She had always been able to sit for hours at a time in contented silence as long as she could exercise her mind. Cilla O'Roarke, she mused, was a different matter. The woman hadn't mastered the fine art of relaxation. Althea filled the squares with her neat, precise printing and thought that Boyd was just the man to teach her how it was done.

Right now, Cilla was bursting to talk. Not to ask questions, Althea thought. She hadn't missed the quick disappointment on Cilla's face when Boyd hadn't been the one to drive her to the station for her night shift.

She's dying to ask me where he is and what he's doing, Althea thought as she filled in the next word. But she doesn't want me to think it matters.

It wasn't possible for her not to smile to herself. Boyd had been pretty closemouthed himself lately. Althea knew he had run a more detailed check on Cilla's background and that he had found answers that disturbed him. Personally, she thought. Whatever he had discovered had nothing to do with the case or he would have shared it with his partner.

But, no matter how close they were, their privacy was deeply respected. She didn't question him. If and when he wanted to talk it through, she would be there for him. As he would be there for her.

It was too bad, she decided, that when sexual tension reared its head, men and women lost that easy camaraderie.

Abruptly Cilla pushed away from the console. "I'm going to get some coffee. Do you want some?"

"Doesn't Nick usually bring some in?"

"He's got the night off."

"Why don't I get it?"

"No." Restlessness seemed to vibrate from her. "I've got nearly seven minutes before the tape ends. I want to stretch my legs."

"All right."

Cilla walked to the lounge. Billy had already been there, she noted. The floor gleamed, and the coffee mugs were washed and stacked. There was the lingering scent of the pine cleaner he always used so lavishly.

She poured two cups and as an afterthought stuck one leftover and rapidly hardening pastry in her pocket.

With a cup in each hand, she turned. In the doorway she saw the shadow of a man. And the silver gleam of a knife. With a scream, she sent the mugs flying. Crockery smashed and shattered.

"Miss O'Roarke?" Billy took a hesitant step into the light.

"Oh, God." She pressed the heel of one hand to her chest as if to force out the air trapped there. "Billy. I thought you were gone."

"I—" He stumbled back against the door when Althea came flying down the hallway, her weapon drawn. In an automatic response, he threw his hands up. "Don't shoot. Don't. I didn't do nothing."

"It's my fault," Cilla said quickly. She stepped over to put a reassuring hand on Billy's arm. "I didn't know anyone was here, and I turned around—" She covered her face with her hands. "I'm sorry," she managed, dropping them again. "I overreacted. I didn't know Billy was still in the station."

"Mr. Harrison had a lunch meeting in his office." He spoke quickly, his eyes darting from Althea to Cilla. "I was just getting to it." He swallowed audibly. "Lots of—lots of knives and forks left over."

Cilla stared at the handful of flatware he held and felt like a fool. "I'm sorry, Billy. I must have scared you to death. And I've made a mess of your floor."

"That's okay." He grinned at her, relaxing slowly as Althea holstered her weapon. "I'll clean it right up. Good show tonight, Miss O'Roarke." He tapped the headphones that he'd slid around his neck. "You going to play any fifties stuff? You know I like that the best."

"Sure." Fighting nausea, she made herself smile. "I'll pick something out just for you."

He beamed at her. "You'll say my name on the air?"

"You bet. I've got to get back."

She hurried back to the booth, grateful that Althea was giving her a few moments alone. Things were getting pretty bad when she started jumping at middle-aged maintenance men holding dinner knives.

The best way to get through the nerves was to work, she told herself. Keeping her moves precise, she began to set up for what she called the "power hour" between eleven and midnight.

When Althea came back, bearing coffee, Cilla was inviting her audience to stay tuned for more music. "We've got ten hits in a row coming up. This first one's for my pal Billy. We're going back, way back, all the way back to 1958. It ain't Dennis Quaid. It's the real, the original, the awesome Jerry Lee Lewis with 'Great Balls of Fire.'"

After pulling off her headphones, she gave Althea a wan smile. "I really am sorry."

"In your place I probably would have gone through the roof." Althea offered her a fresh mug. "Been a lousy couple of weeks, huh?"

"The lousiest."

"We're going to get him, Cilla."

"I'm hanging on to that." She chose another record, took her time cuing it up. "What made you become a cop?"

"I guess I wanted to be good at something. This was it."

"Do you have a husband?"

"No." Althea wasn't sure where the questions were leading. "A lot of men are put off when a woman carries a gun." She hesitated, then decided to take the plunge. "You might have gotten the impression that there's something between Boyd and me."

"It's hard not to." Cilla lifted a hand for silence, then opened the mike to link the next song. "You two seem well suited."

As if considering it, Althea sat and sipped at her coffee. "You know, I wouldn't have figured you for the type to fall into the clichéd, sexist mind-set that says that if a man and woman work together they must be playing together."

"I didn't." Outraged, Cilla all but came out of her chair. At Althea's bland smile, she subsided. "I did," she admitted. Then her lips curved. "Kind of. I guess you've had to handle that tired line quite a bit."

"No more than you, I imagine." She gestured, both hands palms out, at the confines of the studio. "An attractive woman in what some conceive of as a man's job."

Even that small patch of common ground helped her to relax. "There was a jock in Richmond who figured I was dying to, ah . . . spin on his turntable."

Understanding and amusement brightened Althea's eyes. "How'd you handle it?"

"During my show I announced that he was hard up for dates and anyone interested should call the station during his shift." She grinned, remembering. "It cooled him off." She turned to her mike to plug the upcoming request line. After an update on the weather, a time check and an intro for the next record, she slipped her headphones off again. "I guess Boyd wouldn't be as easily discouraged."

"Not on your life. He's stubborn. He likes to call it patience, but it's plain mule-headed stubbornness. He can be like a damn bulldog."

"I've noticed."

"He's a nice man, Cilla, one of the best. If you're really not interested, you should make it clear up front. Boyd's stubborn, but he's not obnoxious."

"I don't want to be interested," Cilla murmured. "There's a difference."

"Like night and day. Listen, if the question's too personal, tell me to shut up."

A smile tugged at Cilla's mouth. "You don't have to tell me that twice."

"Okay. Why don't you want to be interested?"

Cilla chose a compact disc, then backed it up with two 45s. "He's a cop."

"So if he was an insurance salesman you'd want to be interested?"

"Yes. No." She let out a huff of breath. Sometimes it was best to be honest. "It would be easier. Then there's the fact that I made a mess of the one serious relationship I've had."

"All by yourself?"

''Mostly.'' She sent out the cut from the CD. ''I'm more comfortable concentrating on my life, and Deborah's. My work and her future.''

''You're not the type that would be happy for long with comfortable.''

''Maybe not.'' She stared down at the phone. ''But I'd settle for it right now.''

So she was running scared, Althea thought as she watched Cilla work. Who wouldn't be? It had to be terrifying to be hounded and threatened by some faceless, nameless man. Yet she was handling it, Althea thought, better than she was handling Boyd and her feelings about him.

She had them, buckets of them. Apparently she just didn't know what to do with them.

Althea kept her silence as the calls began to come in. Cilla was afraid of the phone, afraid of what might be on the other end. But she answered, call after call, moving through them with what sounded like effortless style. If Althea hadn't been in the studio, watching the strain tighten Cilla's face, she would have been totally fooled.

She gave them their music and a few moments of her time. If her hand was unsteady, her finger still pushed the illuminated button.

Boyd had entered her life to protect it, not threaten it. Yet she was afraid of him. With a sigh, Althea wondered why it was that women's lives could be so completely turned upside down by the presence of a man.

If she ever fell in love herself—which so far she'd had the good sense to avoid—she would simply find a way to call the shots.

The tone of Cilla's voice had her snapping back. Recognizing the fear, sympathizing with it, Althea rose to massage her rigid shoulders.

"Keep him talking," she whispered. "Keep him on as long as you can."

Cilla blocked out what he said. She'd found it helped her keep sane if she ignored the vicious threats, the blood-chilling promises. Instead she kept her eye on the elapsed-time clock, grimly pleased when she saw that the one-minute mark had passed and he was still on the line.

She questioned him, forcing herself to keep her voice calm and even. He liked it best when she lost control, she knew. He would keep threatening until she began to beg. Then he would cut her off, satisfied that he had broken her again.

Tonight she struggled not to hear, just to watch the seconds tick away.

"I haven't hurt you," she said. "You know I haven't done anything to you."

"To him." He hissed the words. "He's dead, and it's because of you."

"Who did I hurt? If you'd tell me his name, I—"

"I want you to remember. I want you to say his name before I kill you."

She shut her eyes and tried to fill her head with sound as he described exactly how he intended to kill her.

"He must have been very important to you. You must have loved him."

"He was everything to me. All I had. He was so young. He had his whole life. But you hurt him. You betrayed him. An eye for an eye. Your life for his. Soon. Very soon."

When he cut her off, she turned quickly to send out the next record. She would backsell it, Cilla told herself. Her voice would be strong again afterward. Ignoring the other blinking lights, she pulled out a cigarette.

"They got a trace." Althea replaced the receiver, then moved over to put a hand on Cilla's shoulder. "They got a trace. You did a hell of a job tonight, Cilla."

"Yeah." She closed her eyes. Now all she had to do was get through the next hour and ten minutes. "Will they catch him?"

"We'll know soon. This is the first real break we've had. Just hang on to that."

She wanted to be relieved. Cilla leaned back as Althea drove her home and wondered why she couldn't accept this step as a step forward. They had traced the call. Didn't that mean they would know where he lived? They would have a name, and they would put a face, a person, together with that name.

She would go and see him. She would make herself do that. She would look at that face, into those eyes, and try to find a link between him and whatever she had done in the past to incite that kind of hate.

Then she would try to live with it.

She spotted Boyd's car at the curb in front of her house. He stood on the walk, his coat unbuttoned. Though the calendar claimed it was spring, the night was cold enough for her to see his breath. But not his eyes.

Cilla took a firm grip on the doorhandle, pushed it open. He waited as she moved up the walk toward him.

"Let's go inside."

"I want to know." She saw his eyes now and understood. "You didn't get him."

"No." He glanced toward his partner. Althea saw the frustration held under grim control.

"What happened?"

"It was a phone booth a couple miles from the station. No prints. He'd wiped it clean."

Struggling to hold on for a few more minutes, Cilla nodded. "So we're no closer."

"Yes, we are." He took her hand to warm it in his. "He made his first mistake. He'll make another."

Weary, she looked over her shoulder. Was it just her overworked nerves, or was he out there somewhere, in the shadows, close enough to see? Near enough to hear?

"Come on, let me take you inside. You're cold."

"I'm all right." She couldn't let him come with her. She needed to let go, and for that she needed privacy. "I don't want to talk about any of this tonight. I just want to go to bed. Althea, thanks for the ride, and everything else." She walked quickly to the front door and let herself inside.

"She just needs to work this out," Althea said, placing a hand on his arm.

He wanted to swear, to smash something with his hands. Instead, he stared at the closed door. "She doesn't want to let me help her."

"No, she doesn't." She watched the light switch on upstairs. "Want me to call for a uniform to stake out the house?"

"No, I'll hang around."

"You're off duty, Fletcher."

"Right. We can consider this personal."

"Want some company?"

He shook his head. "No. You need some sleep."

Althea hesitated, then let out a quiet sigh. "You take the first shift. I sleep better in a car than a bed, anyway."

There was a light frost that glittered like glass on the lawn. Cilla sighed as she studied it through her bedroom window. In Georgia the azaleas would be blooming. It had been years, more years than she could remember, since she had yearned for home. In that chill Colorado morning she wondered if she had made a mistake traveling more than halfway across the country and leaving all those places, all those memories of her childhood, behind.

Letting the curtain fall again, she stepped back. She had more to think about than an April frost. She had also seen Boyd's car, still parked at the curb.

Thinking of him, she took more time and more care dressing than was her habit. Not for a moment had she changed her mind about it being unwise to become involved with him. But it seemed it was a mistake she'd already made. The wisdom to face up to her mistakes was something she'd learned very early.

She smoothed her plum-colored cashmere sweater over her hips. It had been a Christmas present from Deborah, and it was certainly more stylish, with its high neck and its generous sleeves, than most of the clothes Cilla chose for herself. She wore it over snug black leggings and on impulse struggled with a pair of star-shaped earrings in glossy silver.

He was spread comfortably over her couch, the newspaper open, a mug of coffee steaming in his hand. His shirt was carelessly unbuttoned to the middle of his chest and wrinkled from being worn all night. His jacket was tossed over the back of the couch, but he still wore his shoulder holster.

She had never known anyone who could melt into his surroundings so easily. At the moment he looked as though he spent every morning of his life in that spot, in her spot, lazily perusing the sports page and drinking a second cup of coffee.

He looked up at her. Though he didn't smile, his utter relaxation was soothing. "Good morning."

"Good morning." Feeling awkward, she crossed to him. She wasn't certain whether she should begin with an apology or an explanation.

"Deborah let me in."

She nodded, then immediately wished she'd worn trousers with pockets. There was nothing to do with her hands but link them together. "You've been here all night."

"Just part of the service."

"You slept in your car."

He tilted his head. Her tone was very close to an accusation. "It wasn't the first time."

"I'm sorry." On a long, shaky breath, she sat on the coffee table across from him. Their knees bumped. He found it a friendly gesture. One of the friendliest she'd made with him. "I should have let you inside. I should have known you would stay. I guess I was—"

"Upset." He passed her his coffee. "You were entitled, Cilla."

"Yeah." She sipped, wincing a bit at the added sugar. "I guess I'd talked myself into believing that you were going to catch him last night. It even—it's weird, but it even unnerved me a bit thinking about finally seeing him, finally knowing the whole story. Then, when we got here and you told me . . . I couldn't talk about it. I just couldn't."

"It's okay."

Her laugh was only a little strained. "Do you have to be so nice to me?"

"Probably not." Reaching out, he touched her cheek. "Would you feel better if I yelled at you?"

"Maybe." Unable to resist, she lifted a hand to his. "I have an easier time fighting than I do being reasonable."

"I've noticed. Have you ever considered taking a day, just to relax?"

"Not really."

"How about today?"

"I was going to catch up with my paperwork. And I have to call a plumber. We've got a leak under the sink." She let her hand fall to her knees, where it moved restlessly. "It's my turn to do the laundry. Tonight I'm spinning records at this class reunion downtown. Bill and Jim are splitting my shift."

"I heard."

"These reunion things . . . they can get pretty wild." She was groping, feeling more foolish by the minute. He'd taken the empty cup and set it aside, and was now holding both of her hands lightly in his. "They can be a lot of fun, though. Maybe you'd like to come and . . . hang around."

"Are you asking me to come and . . . hang around, like on a date?"

"I'll be working," she began, then subsided. She was getting in deep. "Yes. Sort of."

"Okay. Can I sort of pick you up?" –

"By seven," she said. "I have to be there early enough to set up."

"Let's make it six, then. We can have some dinner first."

"I . . ." Deeper and deeper. "All right. Boyd, I have to tell you something."

"I'm listening."

"I still don't want to get involved. Not seriously."

"Mm-hmm."

"You're completely wrong for me."

"That's just one more thing we disagree on." He held her still when she started to rise. "Don't pace, Cilla. Just take a couple deep breaths."

"I think it's important we understand up front how far this can go, and what limitations there are."

"Are we going to have a romance, Cilla, or a business arrangement?"

He smiled. She frowned.

"I don't think we should call it a romance."

"Why not?"

"Because it's . . . because a romance has implications."

He struggled against another smile. She wouldn't appreciate the fact that she amused him. "What kind of implications?" Slowly, watching her, he brought her hand to his lips.

"Just . . ." His mouth brushed over her knuckles, and then, when her fingers went limp, he turned her palm up to press a kiss to its center.

"Just?" he prompted.

"Implications. Boyd—" She shivered when his teeth grazed over her wrist.

"Is that all you wanted to tell me?"

"No. Can you stop that?"

"If I really put my mind to it."

She found that her own lips had curved. "Well, put your mind to it. I can't think."

"Dangerous words." But he stopped nibbling.

"I'm trying to be serious."

"So am I." Once again he stopped her from rising. "Try that deep breath."

"Right." She did, then plunged on. "Last night, when I lay down in the dark, I was afraid. I kept hearing him, hearing that voice, everything he'd said to me. Over and over. I knew I couldn't think of it. If I did, I'd go crazy. So I thought of you." She paused, waiting for the courage to go on. "And when I thought of you it blocked out everything else. And I wasn't afraid."

His fingers tightened on hers. Her eyes were steady, but he saw that her lips trembled once before she pressed them together. She was waiting, he knew. To see what he would do, what he would say. She couldn't have known, couldn't have had any idea, that at that moment, at that one instant of time, he teetered off the edge he'd been walking and tumbled into love with her.

And if he told her that, he thought as he felt the shock of the emotions vibrate through him, she would never believe it. Some women had to be shown, convinced, not merely told. Cilla was one of them.

Slowly he rose, drawing her up with him. He gathered her close, cradling her head on his shoulder, wrapping his arms around her. He could feel her shiver of relief as he kept the embrace quiet and undemanding.

It was just what she needed. How was it he seemed always to know? To be held, only held, without words, without promises. To feel the solid warmth of his body against her, the firm grip of his hands, the steady beat of his heart.

"Boyd?"

"Yeah." He turned his head just enough to kiss her hair.

"Maybe I don't mind you being nice to me after all."

"We'll give it a trial run."

She thought she might as well go all the way with it. "And maybe I've missed having you around."

It was his turn to take a deep breath and steady himself. "Listen." He slid his hands up to her shoulders. "I've got some calls to make. After, why don't I take a look at that leak?"

She smiled. "I can look at it, Slick. What I want is to have it fixed."

He leaned forward and bit her lower lip. "Just get me a wrench."

Two hours later, Cilla had her monthly finances spread out over the secondhand oak desk in the den that doubled as her office. There were two dollars and fifty-three cents lost somewhere in her checkbook, an amount she was determined to find before she paid the neat stack of bills to her right.

Her sense of order was something she'd taught herself, something she'd clung to during the lean years, the unhappy years, the stormy years. If amid any crisis she could maintain this small island of normalcy, however bland, she believed she would survive.

"Ah!" She found the error, pounced on it. Making the correction, she scrupulously ran her figures again.

Satisfied, she filed away her bank statement, then began writing checks, starting with the mortgage.

Even that gave her an enormous sense of accomplishment. It wasn't rent, it was equity. It was hers. The house was the first thing she had ever owned other than the clothes on her back and the occasional secondhand car.

She'd never been poor, but she had learned, growing up in a family where the income was a combination of a cop's salary and the lean monthly earnings of a public defender, to count pennies carefully. She'd grown up in a rented house, and she'd never known the luxury of riding in a new car. College wouldn't have been impossible, but because of the strain it would have added to her parents' income at a time when their marriage was rocky Cilla had decided to bypass her education in favor of a job.

She didn't regret it often. She resented it only a little, at odd times. But her ability to subsidize Deborah's partial scholarship made her look back to the time when she had made the decision. It had been the right one.

Now they were slowly creeping their way up. The house wasn't simply an acquisition, it was a statement. Family, home, roots. Every month, when she paid the mortgage, she was grateful she'd been given the chance.

"Cilla?"

"What? Oh." She spotted Boyd in the doorway. She started to speak again, then focused. He still had the wrench she'd given him. His hair was mussed and damp. Both his shirt and his slacks were streaked with wet. He'd rolled his sleeves up to the elbows. Water glistened on his forearms. "Oh," she said again, and choked on a laugh.

"I fixed it." His eyes narrowed as he watched her struggle to maintain her dignity. "Problem?"

"No. No, not a thing." She cleared her throat. "So, you fixed it."

"That's what I said."

She had to bite down on her lip. She recognized a frazzled male ego when she heard it. "That's what you said, all right. And since you've just saved me a bundle the least I can do is fix you lunch. What do you think about peanut butter and jelly?"

"That it belongs in a plastic lunch box with Spiderman on the outside."

"Well, I've got to tell you, Slick, it's the best thing I cook." Forgetting the bills, she rose. "It's either that or a can of tuna fish." She ran a fingertip down his shirt experimentally. "Did you know you're all wet?"

He held up one grimy hand, thought about it, then went with the impulse and rubbed it all over her face. "Yeah."

She laughed, surprising him. Seducing him. He'd heard that laugh before, over the radio, but not once since he'd met her. It was low and rich and arousing as black silk.

"Come on, Fletcher, we'll throw that shirt in the wash while you eat your sandwich."

"In a minute." He kept his hand cupped on her chin, pulling her to him with that subtle pressure alone. When his mouth met hers, her lips were still curved. This time, she didn't stiffen, she didn't protest. With a sigh of acceptance, she opened for him, allowing herself to absorb the taste of his mouth, the alluring dance of his tongue over hers.

There was a warmth here that she had forgotten to hope for. The warmth of being with someone who understood her. And cared, she realized as his fingers skimmed over her cheek. Cared, despite her flaws.

"I guess you were right," she murmured.

"Damn right. About what?"

She took a chance, an enormous one for her, and brushed at the hair on his forehead. "It is too late."

"Cilla." He brought his hands to her shoulders again, battling back a clawing need, a ragged desire. "Come upstairs with me. I want to be with you."

His words sent the passion leaping. He could see the fire of it glow in her eyes before she closed them and shook her head. "Give me some time. I'm not playing games here, Boyd, but the ground's pretty shaky and I need to think it through." On a steadying breath, she opened her eyes, and nearly smiled. "You're absolutely everything I swore I'd never fall for."

He brought his hands down to hers and gripped. "Talk to me."

"Not now." But she laced her fingers with his. It was a sign of union that was rare for her. "I'm not ready to dig it all up right now. I'd just like to spend a few hours here like real people. If the phone rings, I'm not going to answer it. If someone comes to the door, I'm going to wait until they go away again. All I want to do is fix you a sandwich and wash your shirt. Okay?"

"Sure." He pressed a kiss to her brow. "It's the best offer I've had in years."

## Chapter 7

There was a wall of noise—the backbeat, the bass, the wail of a guitar riff. There were spinning lights, undulating bodies, the clamor of feet. Cilla set the tone with her midnight voice and stood back to enjoy the results. The ballroom was alive with sound—laughter, music, voices raised in spurts of conversation. Cilla had her finger on the controls. She didn't know any of the faces, but it was her party.

Boyd sipped a club soda and politely avoided a none-too-subtle invitation from a six-foot blonde in a skimpy blue dress. He didn't consider this a trial. He'd spent a large portion of his career watching people, and he'd never gotten bored with it.

It was a hell of a party, and he wouldn't have minded a turn on the dance floor. But he preferred keeping his eye on Cilla. There were worse ways to spend the evening.

She presided over a long table at the front of the ballroom, her records stacked, her amps turned up high. She glittered. Her silver-sequined jacket and black stovepipe pants were a whole new look in tuxedos. Her hair was full and loose, and when she turned her head the silver stars at her ears glistened.

She'd already lured dozens of couples onto the dance floor, and they were bopping and swaying elbow to elbow. Others crowded around the edges in groups or loitered at the banquet tables, lingering over drinks and conversation.

The music was loud, hot and fast. He'd already learned that was how she liked it best. As far as he could tell, the class of 75 was having the time of their lives. From all appearances, Cilla was, too.

She was joking with a few members of the graduating class, most of them male. More than a few of them had imbibed freely at the cash bar. But she was handling herself, Boyd noted. Smooth as silk.

He didn't particularly like it when a man with a lineman's chest put a beefy arm around her and squeezed. But Cilla shook her head. Whatever brush-off she used, she sent the guy off with a smile on his face.

"There's more where that came from, boys and girls. Let's take you back, all the way back to prom night, 1975." She cued up the Eagles' "One Of These Nights," then skimmed the crowd for Boyd.

When she spotted him, she smiled. Fully, so that even with the room between them he could see her eyes glow. He wondered if he could manage to get her to look at him like that when they didn't have five hundred people between them. He had to grin when she put a hand to her throat and mimed desperate thirst.

Lord, he looked wonderful, Cilla thought as she watched him turn toward the bar. Strange, she would have thought a smoke-gray jacket would look too conservative on a man for her tastes. On him, it worked. So well, she mused with a wry smile, that half the female portion of the class of 75 had their eye on him.

Tough luck, ladies, she thought. He's mine. At least for tonight.

A little surprised by where her thoughts had landed, she shook herself back and chose a slip from the pile of requests next to the turntable. A nostalgic crowd, she decided and plucked another fifteen-year-old hit from her stack.

She liked working parties, watching people dance and flirt and gossip. The reunion committee had done a top-notch job on this one. Red and white streamers dripped from the ceiling, competing with a hundred matching balloons. The dance floor glittered from the light of a revolving mirror ball. When the music or the mood called for it, she could flick a switch on a strobe light and give them a touch of seventies psychedelia.

Mixed with the scents of perfume and cologne was the fragrance of the fresh flowers that adorned each table.

"This is for Rick and Sue, those high school sweeties who've been married for twelve years. And they said it was only puppy love. We're 'Rockin' All Over The World.'"

"Nice touch," Boyd commented.

She twisted her head and smiled. "Thanks."

He handed her a soft drink heaped with ice. "I've got a reunion coming up next year. You booked?"

"I'll check my schedule. Wow." She watched as a couple cut loose a few feet away. Other couples spread out as they put the dirty in dirty dancing. "Pretty impressive."

"Mmm. Do you dance?"

"Not like that." She let out a little breath. "I wish I did."

He took her hand before she could reach for another request slip. "Why don't you play one for me?"

"Sure. Name it."

When he poked through her discs, she was too amused to be annoyed. She could reorganize later. After choosing one, he handed it to her.

"Excellent taste." She shifted her mike. "We've got ourself a wild group tonight. Y'all having fun?" The roar of agreement rolled across the dance floor. "We're going to be here until midnight, pumping out the music for you. We've got a request here for Springsteen. 'Hungry Heart.'"

Fresh dancers streamed onto the floor. Couples twined around each other to sway. Cilla turned to speak to Boyd and found herself molded against him.

"Want to dance?" he murmured.

They already were. Body fitted to body, he took her on a long, erotically slow circle. "I'm working."

"Take five." He lowered his head to catch her chin between his teeth. "Until I make love with you, this is the next best thing."

She was going to object. She was sure of it. But she was moving with him, her body fine-tuned to his. In silent capitulation, she slid her arms around his neck. With their faces close, he smiled. Slowly, firmly, he ran his hands over her hips, up, lazily up to the sides of her breasts, then down again.

She felt as though she'd been struck by lightning.

"You've, ah, got some nice moves, Slick."

"Thanks." When their lips were a whisper apart, he shifted, leaving hers hungry as he nuzzled into her neck. "You smell like sin, Cilla. It's just one of the things about you that's been driving me crazy for days."

She wanted him to kiss her. Craved it. She moaned when his hands roamed into her hair, drawing her head back. Her eyes closed in anticipation, but he only brushed those tempting lips over her cheekbone.

Breathless, she clung to him, trying to fight through the fog of pleasure. There were hundreds of people around them, all moving to the erotic beat of the music. She was working, she reminded herself. She was— had always been—a sensible woman, and tonight she had a job to do.

"If you keep this up, I won't be able to work the turntable."

He felt her heart hammering against his. It wasn't enough to satisfy him. But it was enough to give him hope. "Then I guess we'll have to finish the dance later."

When he released her, Cilla turned quickly and chose a record at random. A cheer went up as the beat pounded out. She lifted the hair from the back of her neck to cool it. The press of bodies—or the press of one body—had driven the temperature up. She'd never realized what a dangerous pastime dancing could be.

"Want another drink?" Boyd asked when she drained her glass.

"No. I'm okay." Steadying herself, she reached for the request sheet on top of her pile. "This is a nice group," she said as she glanced across the room. "I like reunions."

"I think I figured that out."

"Well, I do. I like the continuity of them. I like seeing all these people who shared the same experience, the same little block of time. 1975," she mused, the paper dangling from her fingers. "Not the greatest era for music, with the dreaded disco onslaught, but there were a few bright lights. The Doobie Brothers were still together. So were the Eagles."

"Do you always measure time in rock and roll?"

She had to laugh. "Occupational hazard. Anyway, it's a good barometer." Tossing her hair back, she grinned at him. "The first record I spun, as a professional, was the Stones' 'Emotional Rescue.' That was the year Reagan was elected the first time, the year John Lennon was shot—and the year the Empire struck back."

"Not bad, O'Roarke."

"It's better than not bad." She considered him. "I bet you remember what was playing on the radio the first time you talked a girl into the back seat of your car."

"'Dueling Banjos.'"

"You're kidding."

"You asked."

She was chuckling as she opened the request sheet. Her laughter died. She thought for a moment her heart had stopped. Carefully she squeezed her eyes shut. But when she opened them again the boldly printed words remained.

I want you to scream when I kill you.

"Cilla?"

With a brisk shake of her head, she passed the note to Boyd.

He was here, she thought, panic clawing as she searched the room. Somewhere in this crowd of laughing, chattering couples, he was watching. And waiting.

He'd come close. Close enough to lay that innocent-looking slip of paper on her table. Close enough to look into her eyes, maybe to smile. He might have spoken to her. And she hadn't known. She hadn't recognized him. She hadn't understood.

"Cilla."

She jolted when Boyd put a hand to her shoulder, and she would have stumbled backward if he hadn't balanced her. "Oh, God. I thought that tonight, just this one night, he'd leave me alone."

"Take a break."

"I can't." Dazed, she clamped her hands together and stared around the room. "I have to—"

"I need to make a call," he told her. "I want you where I can see you."

He could still be here, she thought. Close enough to touch her. Did he have the knife? The long-bladed knife he'd so lovingly described to her? Was he waiting for the moment when the music was loud, when the laughter was at a peak, so that he could plunge it into her?

"Come on."

"Wait. Wait a minute." With her nails biting into her palms, she leaned into the mike. "We're going to take a short break, but don't cool down. I'll be back in ten to start things rocking again." Mechanically she shut off her equipment. "Stay close, will you?" she whispered.

With an arm snug around her waist, he began to lead her through the crowd. Every time they were bumped she shuddered. When a man pushed through the throng and grabbed both of her hands, she nearly screamed.

"Cilla O'Roarke." He had a pleasant, affable face dampened with sweat from a turn on the dance floor. He was beaming as Cilla stood as still as a statue and Boyd tensed beside her. "Tom Collins. Not the drink," he said, still beaming. "That's my name. I'm chairman of the reunion committee. Remember?"

"Oh." She forced her lips to curve. "Yes. Sure."

"Just wanted to tell you how thrilled we are to have you. Got a lot of fans here." He released one of her hands to sweep his arm out. "I'm about the biggest. There's hardly a night goes by I don't catch at least a part of your show. Lost my wife last year."

"I . . ." She cleared her throat. "I'm sorry."

"No, I mean I lost her. Came home one night and she and the furniture were gone. Never did find her—or the sectional sofa." He laughed heartily while Cilla searched for something to say. "Fact is, your show got me through some pretty lonely nights. Just wanted to thank you and tell you you're doing a hell of a job here tonight." He pressed a business card into her hand. "I'm in appliances. You just call me whenever you need a new refrigerator." He winked. "Give you a good deal."

"Thanks." It should be funny, she thought. Later it would be funny. "Nice seeing you, Tom."

"Pleasure's mine." He watched her walk away and beamed again.

Boyd steered her out of the ballroom and toward the nearest pay phone. "Hang on. Okay?"

She nodded, even managed to smile at a group of women herding toward the ladies' lounge. "I'm better now. I'm going to sit down right over there." She pointed to an arrangement of chairs and a potted plant.

Leaving Boyd digging for change, she walked over, then let her legs collapse under her.

It was a nightmare. She wished it was as simple as a nightmare so that she could wake up with the sun shining in her face. She had nearly gotten through an entire day without thinking of him.

Shaky, she pulled out a cigarette.

Perhaps it had been foolish to let herself believe he would give her a day of peace. But to have come here. The odds of him actually being one of the alumni were slim. Yet he'd gotten inside.

With her back pressed into the chair, she watched people file in and out of the ballroom. It could be any one of them, she thought, straining for some spark of recognition. Would she know him if she saw him, or would he be a complete stranger?

He could be someone standing behind her at the market, someone sitting across from her at a gas pump. He might be the man in front of her at the bank, or the clerk at the dry cleaners.

Anyone, she thought as she closed her eyes. He could be any one of the nameless, faceless people she passed in the course of a day.

Yet he knew her name. He knew her face. He had taken away her peace of mind, her freedom. He wouldn't be satisfied until he'd taken her life.

She watched Boyd hang up the phone and waited until he crossed to her. "Well?"

"Thea's coming by to pick up the paper. We'll send it to the lab." His hand found the tensed muscle at the curve of her neck and soothed. "I don't think we'll get prints."

"No." She appreciated the fact that he didn't give her any false hope. "Do you think he's still here?"

"I don't know." That was its own frustration. "It's a big hotel, Cilla. There's no security to speak of for this event. It wouldn't be very effective to try to close it off and interrogate everyone in it. If you want to take off early, I can tell them you're sick."

"No, I don't want to do that." She took a long last drag on her cigarette. "The only satisfaction I can get is from finishing out. Proving I'm not ready to fold. Especially if he *is* still around, somewhere."

"Okay. Remember, for the next hour, I'm never going to be more than a foot away."

She put a hand in his as she rose. "Boyd, he changed his approach, writing a note. What do you think it means?"

"It could mean a lot of things."

"Such as?"

"Such as it was the most convenient way to contact you tonight. Or he's starting to get sloppy."

"Or impatient," she added, turning to him at the doorway. "Be honest with me."

"Or impatient." He cupped her face in his hands. "He has to get through me first, Cilla. I can promise that won't be an easy job."

She made herself smile. "Cops like to think they're tough."

"No." He kissed her lightly. "Cops have to be tough. Come on. Maybe you've got 'Dueling Banjos' in there. You can play it for me for old times' sake."

"Not on a bet."

She got through it. He'd never doubted that she would, and yet the way she held on despite her fears amazed and impressed him. Not once did she bog down, break down or falter. But he saw the way she studied the crowd, searched the faces as the music raged around her.

Her hands moved constantly, tapping out the beat on the table, shifting through records, fiddling with the sequined studs on her pleated shirt.

She would never be serene, he thought. She would never be soothing. She would pace her way through life driven by nerves and ambition. She would make a demanding and unsettling companion.

Not what he'd had in mind on the rare occasions he'd considered marriage and family. Not even close, he realized with a faint smile. But she was exactly what he wanted and intended to have.

He would protect her with his life. That was duty. He would cherish her for a lifetime. That was love. If the plans he'd made ran smoothly, she would understand the difference very soon.

He, too, was searching the crowd, studying the faces, watching for any sign, any movement, that would bring that quick tensing of the gut called instinct. But the music raged on. The partygoers laughed.

He saw Althea enter. And so, he thought with a shake of his head, did most of the men in the room. He had to chuckle when he saw one woman jab her husband in the ribs as he gawked at the redhead skirting the dance floor.

"You always make an entrance, Thea."

She only shrugged. She was wearing a simple off-the-shoulder cocktail dress in basic black. "I should thank you for getting me out of what turned into an annoying evening. My date had a toothbrush in his pocket and a night of wild sex on his mind."

"Animal."

"Aren't they all?" She glanced past him to Cilla. Amusement faded, to be replaced by concern. "How's she holding up?"

"She's incredible."

She lifted one arched brow. "Partner, my sharp investigative skills lead me to believe that you are seriously infatuated with our assignment."

"I passed infatuation. I'm in love with her."

Thea's lips formed a thoughtful pout. "Is that with a lowercase or uppercase *L*?"

"That's in all caps." He looked away from Cilla to his partner. There were few others with whom he would share his private thoughts. "I'm thinking marriage, Thea. Want to be my best man?"

"You can count on me." Still, she laid a hand on his arm. "I don't want to be a drag, Boyd, but you've got to keep some perspective on this. The lady's in trouble."

He struggled against annoyance. "I can function as a cop and as a man." Because it wasn't something he wanted to discuss at length, he reached in his pocket. "Here's the note, for what it's worth."

She skimmed the message, then slipped it into her bag. "We'll see what the lab boys can do."

He only nodded. "The ex-husband looks clean." An enormous disappointment. "I finished running him through tonight. State Senator Lomax has been married for seven years, and has one point six children. He hasn't been out of Atlanta for three months."

"I finally got ahold of the station manager in Chicago. He had nothing but good things to say about Cilla. I checked out his story about being in Rochester the past week visiting his daughter. It pans. She had a girl. Seven pounds, six ounces. He faxed me the personnel files on the jocks and staff who were at the station when Cilla worked there. So far nothing."

"When I come in Monday, we'll take a closer look."

"I figured I'd go over the file this weekend. Stick close to our girl."

"I owe you one, Thea."

"You owe me more than one, but who's counting?" She started out, pausing once, then twice, to refuse the offer of a dance. Then, again, to decline a more intimate offer.

Because a party was appreciated more when it ended on a fever pitch, Cilla chose the last three songs for their beat rather than their sentiment. Jackets were off, ties were undone and careful hairstyles were limp. When the last song ended, the dance floor was jammed.

"Thank you, class of 75, you've been great. I want to see all of you back here for your twentieth."

"Good job," Boyd told her.

She was already stacking records as the crowd split off into groups. Phone numbers and addresses would be exchanged. A few of the goodbyes would be tearful. "It's not over yet."

It helped to work. She had to break down the equipment, and with the help of the hotel staff she would load it into Boyd's car. Then there would be a trip back to the station and the unloading. After that, maybe she would allow herself to think again.

"It *was* a good job."

She looked up, surprised. "Mark? What are you doing here?"

"I could say I was checking up on one of my jocks." He picked up one of the 45s and laughed. "God, don't tell me you actually played this."

"It was pretty hot in 75." Suspicious, she took it back from him. "Now, why don't you tell me what you're really doing here?"

Feeling nostalgic himself, he glanced around. He and his wife had met in high school. "I'm here to get my equipment."

"Since when does the station manager load equipment?"

"I'm the boss," he reminded her. "I can do whatever I want. And as of now..." He glanced casually at his watch. "You're on sick leave."

It was suddenly very clear. She shot an accusing look at Boyd. "I'm not sick."

"You are if I say you are," Mark countered. "If I see you at the station before your shift Monday night, you're fired."

"Damn it, Mark."

"Take it or leave it." Softening the blow, he put his hands on her shoulders. "It's business, Cilla. I've had jocks burn out from a lot less pressure than you're under. I want you for the long haul. And it's personal. You've got a lot of people worried about you."

"I'm handling it."

"Then you should be able to handle a couple of free days. Now get out of here."

"But who's going to—"

Boyd took her arm. "You heard the man."

"I hate being bullied," she muttered as he dragged her along.

"Too bad. I guess you figure KHIP is going to fall apart without you there for a weekend."

Without turning her head, she shifted her eyes and aimed a killing look at him. "That's not the point."

"No, the point is you need a rest, and you're going to get it."

She grabbed her coat before he could help her on with it. "Just what the hell am I supposed to do with myself?"

"We'll think of something."

Seething with resentment, she stalked out to the parking lot. A few stragglers from the reunion loitered around their cars. She plopped into the passenger's seat and scowled.

"Since when did *we* come into it?"

"Since, by an odd coincidence, I've also got the weekend off."

Eyes narrowed, she studied him as he conscientiously buckled her seat belt. "It smells like a conspiracy."

"You haven't seen anything yet."

He deliberately chose a cassette of classical music and popped it into the tape player before driving out of the lot.

"Mozart?" she said with a sneer.

"Bach. It's called cleansing the palate."

On a heavy sigh, she reached for a cigarette. She didn't want people worried about her, didn't want to admit she was tired. Wasn't ready to admit she was relieved. "This stuff always puts me to sleep."

"You could use the rest."

She had her teeth clenched as she punched in the lighter. "I don't appreciate you running to Mark this way."

"I didn't run to Mark. I simply called him and suggested you could use some time."

"I can take care of myself, Slick."

"Your taxes are being used to see that I take care of you."

"Have I mentioned lately how much I dislike cops?"

"Not in the past twenty-four hours."

Apparently he wasn't going to rise to any of the bait she dangled and allow her to purge her annoyance with a fight. Maybe it was for the best after all, she decided. She could use the time to catch up on her reading. The last two issues of *Radio and Records* were waiting for her attention. She also wanted to look through one of the garden magazines that had come in the mail. It would be nice to plant some summer flowers around the house, maybe some bushes. She hadn't a clue what sort of thing suited Denver's climate.

The idea made her smile. She would buy a window box, and maybe one of those hanging baskets. Perhaps that was why she didn't notice they were heading in the wrong direction until Boyd had been driving for twenty minutes.

"Where are we?" She sat up quickly, blinking.

"On 70, heading west."

"Highway 70? What the devil are we doing on 70?"

"Driving to the mountains."

"The mountains." Groggy, she pushed back her tumbled hair. "What mountains?"

"I think they're called the Rockies," he said dryly. "You might have heard of them."

"Don't get smart with me. You're supposed to be driving me home."

"I am—in a manner of speaking. I'm driving you to my home."

"I've seen your home." She jerked her thumb. "It's back that way."

"That's where I live in Denver. This is the place I have in the mountains. It's a very comfortable little cabin. Nice view. We're going for the weekend."

"*We* are not going anywhere for the weekend." She shifted in her seat to glare at him. "I'm spending the weekend at home."

"We'll do that next weekend," he said, perfectly reasonable.

"Look, Fletcher, as a cop you should know when you take somebody somewhere against their will it's considered a crime."

"You can file charges when we get back."

"Okay, this has gone far enough." It wouldn't do any good to lose her temper, she reminded herself. He was immune. "You might think you're doing this for my own good, but there are other people involved. There's no way I'm going to leave Deborah in that house alone while this maniac is running loose looking for me."

"Good point." He glided off at an exit and nearly had her relaxing. "That's why she's spending a couple of days with Althea."

"I—"

"She told me to tell you to have a good time. Oh," he continued while Cilla made incoherent noises, "she packed a bag for you. It's in the trunk."

"Just when did you plan all this?" That fabulous voice of hers was quiet. Too quiet, Boyd decided, bracing for the storm.

"I had some free time today. You'll like the cabin. It's peaceful, not too remote, and like I said, it has a nice view."

"As long as there's a nice high cliff I can throw you off of."

He slowed to navigate the winding road. "There's that, too."

"I knew you had nerve, Fletcher, but this goes beyond. What the hell made you think you could just put me in a car, arrange my sister's life and drive me off to some cabin?"

"Must've had a brainstorm."

"Brain damage is more like it. Get this straight. I don't like the country, I don't like rustic. I am not a happy camper, and I won't go."

"You're already going."

How could he stay so irritatingly calm? "If you don't take me back, right now, I'm going to—"

"What?"

She ground her teeth. "You have to sleep sometime." Her own words made her take a quantum leap. "You creep," she began on a fresh wave of fury. "If this is your way of getting me into bed, you miscalculated. I'll sit in the car and freeze first."

"There's more than one bedroom in the cabin," he said mildly. "You're welcome to share mine, or take any of the others. It's your choice."

She slumped back in her seat, finally speechless.

## Chapter 8

She didn't intend to romanticize it. Being swept away was fine in books about titled ladies and swaggering buccaneers. But it didn't play well in twentieth-century Denver.

She didn't intend to change her attitude. If the only revenge available to her was keeping a frosty distance, she would keep it very well. He wouldn't get one smile or one kind word until the entire ridiculous weekend was over.

That was why it was a shame that her first glimpse of the house was in the moonlight.

He called this a cabin? Cilla was grateful the music masked her surprised gasp. Her idea of a cabin was a squat little log structure in the middle of nowhere lacking all possible conveniences. The kind of place men went when they wanted to grow beards, drink beer and complain about women.

It was built of wood—a soft, aged wood that glowed warm in the dappled moonlight. But it was far from little. Multileveled, with interesting juts of timber and windows, it rested majestically amid the snow-dusted pine. Decks, some covered, some open, promised a breathtaking view from any direction. The metal roof glinted, making her wonder how it would be to sit inside and listen to rain falling.

But she stubbornly bit back all the words of praise and pushed out of the car. The snow came up to mid-calf and clogged in her shoes.

"Great," she muttered. Leaving him to deal with whatever luggage they had, she trudged up to the porch.

So it was beautiful, she thought. It didn't make any difference. She still didn't want to be there. But since she was, and hailing a cab wasn't a possibility, she would keep her mouth shut, choose the bedroom farthest away from his and crawl into bed. Maybe she'd stay there for forty-eight hours.

Cilla kept the first part of the vow when he joined her on the porch. The only sounds were the planks creaking under his weight and the calling of something wild in the woods. After setting their bags aside, he unlocked the door and gestured her inside.

It was dark. And freezing. Somehow that made her feel better. The more uncomfortable it was, the more justified her foul temper. Then he switched on the lights. She could only gape.

The main room at the cabin's center was huge, an open gabled structure with rough-hewn beams and a charming granite fireplace. Thick, cushy furniture was arranged around it. Its freestanding chimney rose up through the high, lofted ceiling. Above, a balcony swept the width of the room, keeping with the theme of open space and wood. In contrast, the walls were a simple white, accented with glossy built-in shelves and many-paned doors and windows.

This was nothing like the arches and curves of his house in Denver. The cabin was all straight lines and simplicity. The wide planked floors were bare. A set of gleaming steps marched straight to the next level. Beside the fireplace was an open woodbox stacked with split logs. A touch of whimsy was added by grinning brass dragons that served as andirons.

"It warms up pretty quick," Boyd said, figuring she would start talking to him again when she was ready. He flipped on the heat before he shucked off his coat and hung it on a mirrored rack just inside the door. Leaving her where she was, he crossed to the fireplace and proceeded to arrange kindling and logs.

"The kitchen's through there." He gestured as he touched a match to some crumpled newspaper. "The pantry's stocked, if you're hungry."

She was, but she'd be damned if she'd admit it. She'd been getting a perverse pleasure in watching her breath puff out in front of her. Sulking, she watched the flames rise up to lick at the logs. He even did that well, she thought in disgust. He'd probably been an Eagle Scout.

When she didn't respond, he stood up, brushing off his hands. As stubborn as she was, he figured he could outlast her. "If you'd rather just go to bed, there are four bedrooms upstairs. Not counting the sleeping porch. But it's a little cold yet to try that."

She knew when she was being laughed at. Setting her chin, she snatched up her bag and stalked up the stairs.

It was hard to tell which room was his. They were all beautifully decorated and inviting. Cilla chose the smallest. Though she hated to admit it, it was charming, with its angled ceiling, its tiny paneled bath and its atrium doors. Dropping her bag on the narrow bed, she dug in to see just what her sister—a partner in this crime—had packed.

The big, bulky sweater and thick cords met with approval, as did the sturdy boots and rag socks. The bag of toiletries and cosmetics was a plus, though she doubted she'd waste her time with mascara or perfume. Instead of her Broncos jersey and frayed chenille robe, there was a swatch of black silk with a matching—and very sheer—peignoir. Pinned to the bodice was a note.

Happy birthday a few weeks early. See you Monday.

Love, Deborah

Cilla blew out a long breath. Her own sister, she thought. Her own baby sister. Gingerly she held up the transparent silk. Just what had Deborah had in mind when she'd packed an outfit like this? she wondered. Maybe that question was best left unanswered. So she'd sleep in the sweater, Cilla decided, but she couldn't resist running her fingertips over the silk.

It felt . . . well, glorious, she admitted. Rarely did she indulge herself with anything so impractical. A small section of her closet was devoted to outfits like the one she'd worn to the reunion. She thought of them more as costumes than as clothes. The rest were practical, comfortable.

Deborah shouldn't have been so extravagant, she thought. But it was so like her. With a sigh, Cilla let the silk slide through her hands.

It probably wouldn't hurt just to try it on. After all, it was a gift. And no one was going to see it.

Heat was beginning to pour through the vents. Grateful, she slipped out of her coat and kicked off her shoes. She'd indulge herself with a hot bath in that cute claw-footed tub, and then she'd crawl under that very comfortable looking quilt and go to sleep.

She meant to. Really. But the hot water lulled her. The package of bubble bath Deborah had tucked in the case had been irresistible. Now the night-spice fragrance enveloped her. She nearly dozed off, dreaming, with the frothy, perfumed water lapping over her skin.

Then there was the skylight over the tub, that small square of glass that let the stardust sprinkle through. Indulgent, Cilla thought with a sigh as she sank deeper in the tub. Romantic. Almost sinfully soothing.

It had probably been silly to light the pair of candles that sat in the deep windowsill instead of using the overhead lamp. But it had been too tempting. And as she soaked and dreamed, their scent wafted around her.

She was just making the best of a bad situation, she assured herself as she rose lazily from the tub. Unpinning her hair, she let it swing around her shoulders as she slipped into the teddy Deborah had given her.

It had hardly any back at all, she noted, just a silly little flounce that barely covered the essentials. It laced up the front, thin, glossy ribbons that crisscrossed and ended in a small bow in the center, just below her breasts. Though it barely covered them, as well, some clever structural secret lifted them up, made them look fuller.

Despite her best intentions, she traced a fingertip down the ribbons, wondering what it would be like to have Boyd unlace them. Imagining what it might be like to have his fingers brush over her just-pampered skin. Would he go slowly, one careful hook at a time, or would he simply tear at them until—

Oh Lord.

Cursing herself, she yanked open the door and dashed out of the steamy bath.

It was ridiculous to daydream that way, she reminded herself. She had never been a daydreamer. Always, always, she had known where she was going and how to get there. Not since childhood had she wasted time with fantasies that had no connection with ambition or success.

She certainly had no business fantasizing about a man, no matter how attracted she was to him, when she knew there was no possible way they could become a comfortable reality.

She would go to bed. She would shut off her mind. And she would pray that she could shut off these needs that were eating away at her. Before she could shove her bag on the floor, she saw the glass beside the bed.

It was a long-stemmed crystal glass, filled with some pale golden liquid. As she sampled it, she shut her eyes. Wine, she realized. Wonderfully smooth. Probably French. Turning, she saw herself reflected in the cheval glass in the corner.

Her eyes were dark, and her skin was flushed. She looked too soft, too yielding, too pliant. What was he doing to her? she asked herself. And why was it working?

Before she could change her mind, she slipped the thin silk over her shoulders and went to find him.

He'd been reading the same page for nearly an hour. Thinking about her. Cursing her. Wanting her. It had taken every ounce of self-possession he had to set that wine beside her bed and leave the room when he could hear her splashing lazily in the tub just one narrow door away.

It wasn't as if it were all one-sided, he thought in disgust. He knew when a woman was interested. It wasn't as if it were all physical. He was in love with her, damn it. And if she was too stupid to see that, then he'd just have to beat her over the head with it.

Laying the book on his lap, he listened to the bluesy eloquence of Billie Holiday and stared into the fire. The cheerful flames had cut the chill in the bedroom. That was the practical reason he had built a fire in here, as well as one on the main floor. But there was another, a romantic one. He was annoyed that he had daydreamed of Cilla as he set the logs and lit the kindling.

She had come to him, wearing something thin, flowing, seductive. She had smiled, held out her hands. Melted against him. When he had lifted her into his arms, carried her to the bed, they had . . .

Keep dreaming, he told himself. The day Cilla O'Roarke came to him of her own free will, with a smile and an open hand, would be the day they built snowmen in hell.

She had feelings for him, damn it. Plenty of them. And if she weren't so bullheaded, so determined to lock up all that incredible passion, she wouldn't spend so much time biting her nails and lighting cigarettes.

Resentful, restrictive and repressed, that was Priscilla Alice O'Roarke, he thought grimly. He picked up his wine for a mock toast. It nearly slid out of his hand when he saw her standing in the doorway.

"I want to talk to you." She'd lost most of her nerve on the short trip down the hall, but she managed to step into the room. She wasn't going to let the fact that he was sitting in front of a sizzling fire wearing nothing but baggy sweats intimidate her.

He needed a drink. After a gulp of wine, he managed a nod. He was almost ready to believe he was dreaming again—but she wasn't smiling. "Yeah?"

She was going to speak, she reminded herself. Say what was on her mind and clear the air. But she needed a sip of her own wine first. "I realize your motives in bringing me here tonight were basically well-intentioned, given the circumstances of the last couple of weeks. But your methods were unbelievably arrogant." She wondered if she sounded like as much of a fool to him as she did to herself. She waited for a response, but he just continued to stare blankly at her. "Boyd?"

He shook his head. "What?"

"Don't you have anything to say?"

"About what?"

A low sound of frustration rumbled in her throat as she stepped closer. She slammed the glass down on a table, and the remaining wine lapped close to the rim. "The least you can do after dragging me all the way up here is to listen when I complain about it."

He was barely capable of breathing, much less listening. In self-defense he took another long sip of wine. "If you had any legs—brains," he corrected, gnashing his teeth, "you'd know that a couple days away from everything would be good for you."

Anger flared in her eyes, making her all the more arousing. Behind her the flames shot high, and the light rippled through the thin silk she wore. "So you just took it on yourself to make the decision for me."

"That's right." In one jerky movement, he set the glass aside to keep it from shattering in his fingers. "If I had asked you to come here for a couple of days, you would have made a dozen excuses why you couldn't."

"We'll never know what I would have done," she countered. "Because you didn't give me the option of making my own choice."

"I'm doing my damnedest to give you the option now," he muttered.

"About what?"

On an oath, he stood up and turned away. Hands braced on the wall, he began, none too gently, to pound his forehead against it. As she watched him, confusion warred with anger.

"What are you doing?"

"I'm beating my head against the wall. What does it look like I'm doing?" He stopped, letting his forehead rest against the wood.

Apparently she wasn't the only one under too much strain, Cilla mused. She cleared her throat. "Boyd, why are you beating your head against the wall?"

He laughed and, rubbing his hands over his face, turned. "I have no idea. It's just something I've felt obliged to do since I met you." She was standing, a little uncertain now, running nervous fingertips up and down her silk lapel. It wasn't easy, but after a deep breath he found a slippery hold on control. "Why don't you go on to bed, Cilla? In the morning you can tear apart what's left of me."

"I don't understand you." She snapped out the words, then began to pace. Boyd opened his mouth but couldn't even manage a groan as he stared at the long length of her back, bare but for the sheerest of black silk, at the agitated swing of her hips, accented by the sassy little flounce. She was talking again, rapid-fire and irritated, but it was all just a buzzing in his head.

"For God's sake, don't pace." He rubbed the heel of his hand against his heart. In another minute, he was sure, it would explode out of his chest. "Are you trying to kill me?"

"I always pace when I'm mad," she tossed back. "How do you expect me to go quietly to bed after you've got me worked up this way?"

"Got you worked up?" he repeated. Something snapped—he would have sworn he heard it boomerang in his head as he reached out and snatched her arms. "I've got you worked up? That's rich, O'Roarke. Tell me, did you wear this thing in here tonight to make me suffer?"

"I . . ." She looked down at herself, then shifted uncomfortably. "Deborah packed it. It's all I've got."

"Whoever packed it, it's you who's packed into it. And you're driving me crazy."

"I just thought we should clear all this up." She was going to start stuttering in a minute. "Talk it through, like grown-ups."

"I'm thinking very much like a grown-up at the moment. If you want to talk, there's a chestful of big, thick wool blankets. You can wrap yourself up in one."

She didn't need a blanket. She was already much too warm. If he continued to rub his hands up and down the silk on her arms, the friction was going to cause her skin to burst into flame.

"Maybe I wanted to make you suffer a little."

"It worked." His fingers toyed with the excuse of a robe as it slid from her right shoulder. "Cilla, I'm not going to make this easy on you and drag you to that bed. I'm not saying the idea doesn't appeal to me a great deal. But if we make love, you're going to have to wake up in the morning knowing the choice was yours."

Wasn't that why she had come to him? Hoping he'd take matters out of her hands? That made her a coward—and, in a miserable way, a cheat.

"It's not easy for me."

"It should be." He slid his hands down to hers. "If you're ready."

She lifted her head. He was waiting—every bit as edgy as she, but waiting. "I guess I've been ready since I met you."

A tremor worked through him, and he struggled against his self-imposed leash. "Just say yes."

Saying it wasn't enough, she thought. When something was important, it took more than one simple word.

"Let go of my hands, please."

He held them another long moment, searching her face. Slowly his fingers relaxed and dropped away from hers. Before he could back up, she moved into him, wrapping her arms around his neck. "I want you, Boyd. I want to be with you tonight."

She brought her lips to his. There had already been enough words. Warm and willing, she sank into him.

For a moment, he couldn't breathe. The onslaught on his senses was too overwhelming. Her taste, her scent, the texture of silk against silk. There was her sigh as she rubbed her lips over his.

He remembered taking a kick in the solar plexus from one of his father's prized stallions. This left him just as debilitated. He wanted to savor, to drown, to lose himself, inch by glorious inch. But even as he slipped the robe from her shoulders she was pulling him to the bed.

She was like a whirlwind, hands racing, pressing, tugging, followed by the mad, erotic journey of her mouth. The pressure was building too fast, but when he reached for her she shimmied out of the silk and rushed on.

She didn't want him to regret wanting her. She couldn't have borne it. If she was to throw every shred of caution to the winds for this one night, she needed to know that it would matter. That he would remember.

His skin was hot and damp. She wished she could have lingered over the taste of it, the feel of it under her fingers. But she thought men preferred speed and power.

She heard him groan. It delighted her. When she tugged off his sweats, his hands were in her hair. He was murmuring something—her name, and more—but she couldn't tell. She thought she understood his urgency, the way he pulled her up against him. When he rolled over her, she whispered her agreement and took him inside her.

He stiffened. On an oath, he tried to level himself and draw back. But her hips arched and thrust against him, leaving his body no choice.

Her lips were curved when he lay over her, his face buried in her hair, his breath still shuddering. He wouldn't regret this, she thought, rubbing a soothing hand over his shoulder. And neither would she. It was more than she had ever had before. More than she had ever expected. There had been a warmth when he filled her, and a quiet contentment when she felt him spill into her. She thought how nice it would be to close her eyes and drift off to sleep with his body still warm on hers.

He was cursing himself, steadily. He was enraged by his lack of control, and baffled by the way she had rushed them both from kiss to completion. He'd barely touched her—in more ways than one. Though it was she who had set the pace at a sprint, he knew she hadn't come close to fulfillment.

Struggling for calm, he rolled away from her to stare at the ceiling. She'd set off bombs inside him, and though they had exploded, neither of them had shared the joy.

"Why did you do that?" he asked her.

Her hand paused on its way to stroke his hair. "I don't understand. I thought you wanted to make love."

"I did." He sat up, dragging the hair back from his face. "I thought you did, too."

"But I thought men liked . . ." She let her eyes close as the warmth drained out of her. "I told you I wasn't very good at it."

He swore, ripely enough to have her jolting. Moving quickly, she scrambled out of bed to struggle back into the peignoir.

"Where the hell are you going?"

"To bed." Because her voice was thick with tears, she lowered it. "We can just chalk this up to one more miscalculation." She reached down for her robe and heard the door slam. Bolting up, she saw Boyd turning a key in the lock, then tossing it across the room. "I don't want to stay here with you."

"Too bad. You already made your choice."

She balled up the robe, hugging it to her chest. So he was angry, she thought. And it was the real thing this time. It wouldn't be the first fight she had had about her inadequacies in bed. Old wounds, old doubts, trickled through her until she stood rigid with embarrassment.

"Look, I did the best I could. If it wasn't good enough, fine. Just let me go."

"Wasn't good enough," he repeated. As he stepped forward, she backed up, ramming into the carved footboard. "Somebody ought to bounce you on your head and knock some sense into it. There are two people in a bed, Cilla, and what happens in it is supposed to be mutual. I wasn't looking for a damn technician."

The angry flush died away from her face until it was marble white. Her eyes filled. Pressing his fingers against his own eyes, he swore. He hadn't meant to hurt her, only to show her that he'd wanted a partner.

"You didn't feel anything."

"I did." She rubbed tears from her cheek, infuriated. No one made her cry. No one.

"Then that's a miracle. Cilla, you barely let me touch you. I'm not blaming you." He took another step, but she evaded him. Searching for patience he stood where he was. "I didn't exactly fight you off. I thought—Let's just say by the time I understood it was too late to do anything about it. I'd like to make it up to you."

"There's nothing to make up." She had herself under control again, eyes dry, voice steady. She wanted to die. "We'll just forget it. I want you to unlock the door."

He let out a huff of breath, then shrugged. When he turned to the door, she started to follow. But he only turned off the lights.

"What are you doing?"

"We tried it your way." In the moonlight, he moved across the room to light a candle, then another and another. He turned over the record that sat silent on the turntable, engaged the needle. The trembling cry of a tenor sax filled the room. "Now we try it mine."

She was starting to tremble now, from embarrassment and from fear. "I said I wanted to go to bed."

"Good." He swept her up into his arms. "So do I."

"I've had enough humiliation for one night," she said between her teeth.

She saw something in his eyes, something dark, but his voice was quiet when he spoke. "I'm sorry. I never meant to hurt you."

Though she held herself rigid, he lowered her gently to the bed. With his eyes on hers, he spread out her hair, letting his fingers linger. "I've imagined you here, in the candlelight, with your hair on my pillow." He lowered his lips to brush them across hers. "Moonlight and firelight on your skin. With nothing and no one else but you for miles."

Moved, she turned her head away. She wouldn't be seduced by words and make a fool of herself again. He only smiled and pressed his lips to her throat.

"I love a challenge. I'm going to make love with you, Cilla." He slipped the strap of the peignoir from her shoulder to cruise the slope with his mouth. "I'm going to take you places you've never even dreamed of." He took her hand, pleased that her pulse had quickened. "You shouldn't be afraid to enjoy yourself."

"I'm not."

"You're afraid to relax, to let go, to let someone get close enough to find out what's inside you."

She tried to shift away, but his arms wrapped around her. "We already had sex."

"Yes, we did." He kissed one corner of her mouth, then the other. "Now we're going to make love."

She started to turn her head again, but he cupped her face with his hands. When his mouth came to hers again, her heart leaped into her throat. It was so soft, so tempting. As his fingertips glided across her face, she gave a strangled sigh. He dipped into her parted lips to tease her tongue with his.

"I don't want—" She moaned as his teeth nipped into her bottom lip.

"Tell me what you do want."

"I don't know." Her mind was already hazy. She lifted a hand to push him away, but it only lay limp on his shoulder.

"Then we'll make it multiple-choice." To please himself, and her, he ran a trail of kisses down her throat. "When I'm finished, you can tell me what you like best."

He murmured to her, soft, dreamy words that floated in her head. Then he drugged her with a kiss, long, lazy, luxurious. Though her body had begun to tremble, he barely touched her—just those fingertips stroking along her shoulders, over her face, into her hair.

His tongue slid over the tops of her breasts, just above the fringe of black lace. Her skin was like honey there, he thought, laving the valley between. Her heart jackhammered against him, but when she reached out he took her hands in his.

Taking his time, his devastating time, he inched the lace down with his teeth. She arched up, offering herself, her fingers tensing like wires against his. He only murmured and, leaving a moist trail, eased the other curve of lace down.

His own breathing was short and shallow, but he fought back the urge to take greedily. With teasing openmouthed kisses he circled her, flicking his hot tongue over her rigid nipple until she shuddered and sobbed out his name. On a groan of pleasure, he suckled.

She felt the pressure deep inside, clenching, unclenching, to the rhythm of his clever mouth. Building, layering, growing, until she thought she would die from it.

Her breath was heaving as she writhed beneath him. Her nails dug hard into the backs of his hand as her body bowed, driven up by a knot of sensation. She heard her own cry, her gasp of relief and torment as something shattered inside her. Hot knives that turned to silky butterfly wings. A pain that brought unreasonable pleasure.

As every muscle in her body went lax, he covered her mouth with his. "Good Lord. You're incredible."

"I can't." She brought a hand up to press a palm to her temple. "I can't think."

"Don't. Just feel."

He straddled her. She was prepared for him to take her. He had already given her more than she had ever had. Shown her more than she had ever imagined. He began to unlace the peignoir with infinite care, infinite patience. His eyes were on her face. He loved being able to see everything she felt as it flickered there. Every new sensation, every new emotion. He heard the whisper of silk against her skin as he drew it down. He felt passion vibrate from her as he pressed his mouth to the quivering flesh of her stomach.

Floating, she stroked his hair, let her mind follow where her body so desperately wanted to go. This was heaven, more demanding, more exciting, more erotic, than any paradise she could have dreamed. She could feel the sheets, hot from her own body, tangled beneath her. And the shimmer of silk as it slipped slowly, slowly away. His skin, dampened from pleasure, slid over hers. When her lips parted on a sigh, she could still taste him there, rich and male. Candlelight played against her closed lids.

There was so much to absorb, so much to experience. If it went on forever, it would still end too soon.

She was his now, he knew. Much more his than she had been when he had been plunged inside her. Her body was like a wish, long and slim and pale in the moonlight. Her breath was quick and quiet. And it was his name, only his name, she spoke when he touched her. Her hands flexed on his shoulder, urging him on.

He slid down her legs, taking the silk with him, nibbling everywhere as he went. The scent of her skin was a tormenting delight he could have lingered over endlessly. But her body was restless, poised. He knew she must be aching, even as he was.

He stroked a fingertip up her thigh, along that sensitive flesh, close, so close, to where the heat centered. When he slipped inside her, she was wet and waiting.

The breathless moan came first, and then the magic of his hands had her catapulting up, over a new and higher crest. Stunned by the power of it, she arched against him, shuddering again and again as she climbed. Though her hands clutched at him, he continued to drive her with his mouth, with his clever and relentless fingers, until she shot beyond pleasure to delirium.

Then her arms were around him and they were spinning off together, rolling over on the bed like lightning and thunder. The time for patience was over. The time for greed had begun.

He fought for breath as her hands raced over him. As she had the first time, she ripped away his control. But now she was with him, beat for beat and need for need. He saw her eyes glow, dark with passion, depthless with desire. Her slick skin shimmered with it in the shadowy light.

One last time he brought his mouth down on hers, swallowing her stunned cry, as he thrust himself into her. On a half sob she wrapped her arms and legs around him, locking tight so that they could race toward madness together.

He was exhausted. Weak as a baby. And he was heavy. Using what strength he could find, Boyd rolled, taking Cilla with him so that their positions were reversed. Satisfied, he cradled her head and decided he very much liked the sensation of her body sprawled over his.

She shuddered. He soothed.

"Cold?"

She just shook her head.

Lazy as a cat, he stroked a hand down her naked back. "I might, in an hour or so, find the strength to look for the blankets."

"I'm fine."

But her voice wasn't steady. Frowning, Boyd cupped a hand under her chin and lifted it. He could see a tear glittering on her lashes. "What's this?"

"I'm not crying," she said, almost fiercely.

"Okay. What are you?"

She tried to duck her head again, but he held it firm. "You'll think I'm stupid."

"Probably the only time I couldn't think you were stupid is right after you've turned me inside out." He gave her a quick kiss. "Spill it, O'Roarke."

"It's just that I . . ." She let out an impatient breath. "I didn't think it was supposed to be that way. Not really."

"What way?" His lips curved. Funny, but it seemed he was getting his strength back. Maybe it was the way she was looking at him. Dazed. Embarrassed. Beautiful. "You mean, like good?" He slid his hands down to caress her bottom casually. "Or very good? Maybe you mean terrific. Or astounding."

"You're making fun of me."

"Uh-uh. I was hoping for a compliment. But you don't want to give me one. I figure you're just too stubborn to admit that my way was better than your way. But that's okay. I also figure I can keep you locked in here until you do.''

"Damn it, Boyd, it's not easy for me to explain myself.''

"You don't have to.'' There was no teasing note in his voice now. The look in his eyes made her weak all over again.

"I wanted to tell you that I never...no one's ever made me...'' She gave up. "It was terrific.''

"Yeah.'' He cupped a hand on the back of her head and brought her mouth to his. "Now we're going to shoot for astounding.''

# Chapter 9

Cilla wrapped her arms across her body to ward off the chill and stared out over the pine and rock. Boyd had been right again. The view was incredible.

From this angle she could see the jagged, snow-capped peaks of the circling mountains. Closer, yet still distant, she caught the faint mist of smoke from a chimney. Evergreens stood, sturdy winter veterans, their needles whistling in the rising wind. There was the harsh whisper of an icy stream. She could catch glimpses of the water, just the glint of it in the fading sun.

The shadows were long, with late afternoon casting a cool blue light over the snow. Earlier she had seen a deer nuzzling her nose into it in search of the grass beneath. Now she was alone.

She'd forgotten what it was to feel so at peace. In truth, she wondered if she had ever known. Certainly not since earliest childhood, when she had still believed in fairy tales and happy endings. It had to be too late, when a woman was nearly thirty, to start believing again.

And yet she doubted things would ever be quite the same again.

He had kept his promise. He had taken her places she had never dreamed of. In one exquisitely long night, he had shown her that love meant you could accept as well as offer, take as well as give. She had learned more than the power of lovemaking in Boyd's bed. She had learned the power of intimacy. The comfort and the glory of it. For the first time in years, she had slept deeply and dreamlessly.

She hadn't felt awkward or uncomfortable on waking with him that morning. She had felt calm. Wonderfully calm. It was almost impossible to believe that there was another world apart from this spot. A world of pain and danger and fear.

Yet there was. And it was a world she would have to face again all too soon. She couldn't hide here—not from a man who wanted her dead, nor from her own miserable memories. But wasn't she entitled to a little more time to pretend that nothing else mattered?

It wasn't right. On a sigh, she lifted her face to the dying sun. No matter how she felt—or perhaps because she had come to feel so deeply—she had to be honest with herself, and with Boyd. She wouldn't let what had started between them go any further. Couldn't, she thought, squeezing her eyes tight. It had to be better to let her heart break a little now than to have it smashed later.

He was a good man, she thought. An honest one, a caring one. He was patient, intelligent and dedicated. And he was a cop.

She shivered and held herself more tightly.

There was a scar just under his right shoulder. Front and back, she remembered. From a bullet—that occupational hazard of law enforcement. She hadn't asked, and wouldn't, how he had come by it, when it had happened, or how near death it had taken him.

But neither could she hide from the fact that the scars she bore were as real as his.

She simply could not delude either of them into believing there was a future for them. She should never have allowed it to progress as far as it had. But that was done. They were lovers. And though she knew that was a mistake, she would always be grateful for the time she had had with him.

The logical thing to do would be to discuss the limitations of their relationship. No strings, no obligations. In all likelihood he would appreciate that kind of practicality. If her feelings had grown too far too fast, she would just have to get a grip on them.

She would simply have to talk herself out of being in love.

He found her there, leaning out on the railing as if she were straining to fly out above the pines, above the snowcapped peaks. The nerves were coming back, he noted with some frustration. He wondered if she knew how relaxed she had been that morning when she had stretched against him, waking gradually, turning to him so that they could make slow, lazy love.

Now, when he touched her hair, she jolted before she leaned back against his hand.

"I like your place, Slick."

"I'm glad." He intended to come back here with her, year after year.

Her fingers danced over the railing, then groped in her pockets. "I never asked you if you bought it or had it built."

"Had it built. Even hammered a few nails myself."

"A man of many talents. It's almost a shame to have a place like this only for weekends."

"I've been known to break away for more than that from time to time. And my parents use it now and again."

"Oh. Do they live in Denver?"

"Colorado Springs." He began to massage the tensing muscles in her shoulders. "But they travel a lot. Itchy feet."

"I guess your father was disappointed when you didn't go into the family business."

"No. My sister's carrying on the family tradition."

"Sister?" She glanced over her shoulder. "I didn't know you had a sister."

"There's a lot you don't know." He kissed her lips when they formed into a pout. "She's a real go getter. Tough, high-powered businesswoman. And a hell of a lot better at it than I would have been."

"But aren't they uneasy about you being a cop?"

"I don't think it's a day-to-day worry. You're getting chilled," he said. "Come on inside by the fire."

She went with him, moving inside and down the rear steps into the kitchen. "Mmm... What's that smell?"

"I threw some chili together." He walked over to the center island, where copper pots hung from the ceiling.

Lifting the lid on a pan simmering on the range, he sniffed. "Be ready in about an hour."

"I would have helped you."

"That's okay." He selected a Bordeaux from the wine rack. "You can cook next time."

She made a feeble attempt at a smile. "So you did like my peanut-butter-and-jelly special."

"Just like Mom used to make."

She doubted that his mother had ever made a sandwich in her life. People who had that kind of money also had a houseful of servants. As she stood feeling foolish, he set the wine on the counter to breathe.

"Aren't you going to take off your coat?"

"Oh. Sure." She shrugged out of it and hung it on a hook by the door. "Is there anything you want me to do?"

"Yes. Relax."

"I am."

"You were." Selecting two glasses from above the rack, he examined them. "I'm not sure what has you tied up again, Cilla, but we're going to talk it through this time. Why don't you go sit by the fire? I'll bring out the wine."

If he read her this easily after a matter of weeks, Cilla thought as she went into the living room, how much would he see in a year? She settled on a low cushion near the fire. She wasn't going to think of a year. Or even a month.

When he came in, she offered him a much brighter smile and reached for her wine. "Thanks. It's a good thing I didn't come here before I went house-hunting. I never would have settled on a house without a fireplace."

In silence, he settled beside her. "Look at me," he said at length. "Are you worried about going back to work?"

"No." Then she sighed. "A little. I trust you and Thea, and I know you're doing what you can, but I am scared."

"Do you trust me?"

"I said I did." But she didn't meet his eyes.

He touched a fingertip to her cheek until she faced him again. "Not just as a cop."

She winced, looked away again. "No, not just as a cop."

"And that's the trigger," he mused. "The fact that I am a cop."

"It's none of my business."

"We both know better."

"I don't like it," she said evenly. "I don't expect you to understand."

"I think I do understand." He leaned back against a chair, watching her as he sipped his wine. "I've done some checking, Cilla—necessary to the investigation. But I won't pretend that's the only reason I looked."

"What do you mean?"

"I looked into your background because I need to protect you. And I need to understand you. You told me your mother was a cop. It wasn't hard to track down what happened."

She clutched her glass in both hands and stared straight ahead, into the flames. After all these years, the pain was just as deadly. "So you punched some buttons on your computer and found out my mother was killed. Line of duty. That's what they call it. Line of duty," she repeated, her voice dull. "As if it were part of a job description."

"It is," he said quietly.

There was a flicker of fear in her eyes when she looked at him, then quickly away again. "Yeah. Right. It was just part of her job to be shot that day. Too bad about my father, though. He just happened to be in the wrong place at the wrong time. The old innocent bystander."

"Cilla, nothing's as black-and-white as that. And nothing's that simple."

"Simple?" She laughed and dragged her hair back from her face. "No, the word's *ironic*. The cop and the public defender, who just happen to be married, are going head-to-head over a case. They never agreed. Never once can I remember them looking at any one thing from the same angle. When this happened, they were talking about a separation—again. Just a trial one, they said." With a thoughtful frown, she studied her glass. "Looks like I'm out of wine."

Saying nothing, Boyd poured her more.

"So I guess you read the official report." She swirled the wine, then drank. "They brought this little creep in for interrogation. Three-time loser—armed robbery, assault, drugs. He wanted his lawyer present while the investigating officer questioned him. Talked about making a deal. He knew there wouldn't be any deal. They had him cold, and he was going to do hard time. He had two people to blame for it—in his head, anyway. His lawyer, and the cop who had collared him."

It was painful, still so painful, to remember, to try to picture an event she hadn't seen, one that had so drastically altered her life.

"They caught the guy who smuggled him the gun," she said softly. "He's still doing time." Taking a moment, she soothed her throat with wine. "There they were, sitting across from each other at the table—just as they might have been in our own kitchen—arguing about the law. The sonofabitch took out that smuggled snub-nosed .22 and shot them both."

She looked down at her glass again. "A lot of people lost their jobs over that incident. My parents lost their lives."

"I'm not going to tell you that cops don't die by mistake, unnecessarily, even uselessly."

When she looked at him, her eyes were eloquent. "Good. And I don't want the crap about how proud we're supposed to be of our valiant boys in blue. Damn it, she was my mother."

He hadn't just read the reports, he'd pored over them. The papers had called it a disgrace and a tragedy. The investigation had lasted more than six months, and when it was over eight officials had resigned or been replaced.

But over and above the facts, he remembered a file picture. Cilla, her face blank with grief, standing by the two graves, clutching Deborah's hand in hers.

"It was a horrible way to lose them," he said.

She just shook her head. "Yes. But in most ways I'd already lost my mother the day she joined the force."

"She had an impressive record," Boyd said carefully. "It wasn't easy for a woman back then. And it's always tough on a cop's family."

"How do you know?" she demanded. "You're not the one who sits at home and sweats. From the day I was old enough to understand, I waited for her captain to come to the door and tell us she was dead."

"Cilla, you can't live your life waiting for the worst."

"I lived my life waiting for a mother. The job always came first—it came before Dad, before me, before Deb. She was never there when I needed her." She snatched her hand aside before he could grasp it. "I didn't care if she baked cookies or folded my socks. I just wanted her to be there when I needed her. But her family was never as important as the masses she'd sworn to serve and protect."

"Maybe she was too focused on her career," he began.

"Don't you compare me with her."

His brow rose. "I wasn't going to." Now he took her hand despite her resistance. "It sounds like you are."

"I've had to be focused. She had people who loved her, who needed her, but she never took time to notice. Cops don't have regular hours, she'd say. Cops don't have regular lives."

"I didn't know your mother, and I can't comment on the choices she made, but don't you think it's time to cut it loose and get on with your life?"

"I have. I've done what I had to do. I've done what I've wanted to do."

"And you're scared to death of what you're feeling for me because of my job."

"It's not just a job," she said desperately. "We both know it's not just a job."

"Okay." He nodded. "It's what I do, and what I am. We're going to have to find a way to deal with it."

"It's your life," she said carefully. "I'm not asking you to change anything. I didn't intend to get this involved with you, but I don't regret it."

"Thanks," he muttered, and drained his own glass.

"What I'm trying to say is that if we're reasonable I think we can keep it uncomplicated."

He set his glass aside. "No."

"No what?"

"No, I don't want to be reasonable, and it's already complicated." He gave her a long look that was very close to grim. "I'm in love with you."

He saw the shock. It flashed into her eyes an instant before she jerked back. The color drained away from her face.

"I see that thrills the hell out of you," he muttered. Rising, he heaved a log on the fire and cursed as he watched the sparks fly.

Cilla thought it best to stay exactly where she was. "Love's a real big word, Boyd. We've only known each other a couple of weeks, and not under the most ideal circumstances. I think—"

"I'm damn tired of you thinking." He turned back to face her. "Just tell me what you feel."

"I don't know." That was a lie, one she knew she would hate herself for. She was terrified. And she was thrilled. She was filled with regrets, and hammered by longings. "Boyd, everything that's happened has happened fast. It's as if I haven't had any control, and that makes me uneasy. I didn't want to be involved with you, but I am. I didn't want to care about you, but I do."

"Well, I finally managed to pry that out of you."

"I don't sleep with a man just because he makes me tingle."

"Better and better." He smiled as he lifted her hand to kiss her fingers. "I make you tingle, and you care about me. Marry me."

She tried to jerk her hand free. "This isn't the time for jokes."

"I'm not joking." Suddenly his eyes were very intense. "I'm asking you to marry me."

She heard a log shift in the grate. Saw the flicker of a new flame as it cast light and shadow over his face. His hand was warm and firm on hers, holding, waiting. Her breath seemed to be blocked somewhere beneath her heart. The effort of dragging in air made her dizzy.

"Boyd—"

"I'm in love with you, Cilla." Slowly, his eyes steady on hers, he pulled her closer. "With every part of you." Soft, persuasive, his lips cruised over hers. "I only want fifty or sixty years to show you." His mouth skimmed down her throat as he lowered her to the hearth rug. "Is that too much to ask?"

"No... Yes." Struggling to clear her mind, she pressed a hand against his chest. "Boyd, I'm not going to marry anyone."

"Sure you are." He nibbled lightly at her lips as his hands began to stroke—soothing and exciting at the same time. "You just have to get used to the fact that it's going to be me." He deepened the kiss, lingering over it until her hand lost its resistance and slid to his back. "I'm willing to give you time." His lips curved as her murmured protest hummed against them. "A day or two. Maybe a week."

She shook her head. "I've already made one mistake. I'm not ever going to repeat it."

He caught her chin in his hand in a movement so quick that her eyes flew open. In his eyes was a ripe, raging fury that was rare for him, and all the more dangerous.

"Don't ever compare me with him."

She started to speak, but his fingers tightened once, briefly, and silenced her.

"Don't ever compare what I feel for you with what anyone else has felt."

"I wasn't comparing you." Her heart was hammering against his chest. "It's me. It was my mistake, mine alone. And I'm never going to make another one like it."

"It takes two people, damn it." Enraged, he braced himself over her, then took both her hands in his. "If you want to play it that way, fine. Ask yourself one question, Cilla. Has anyone else made you feel like this?"

His mouth swooped down to take hers in a hot, rough, frantic kiss that had her arching against him. In protest? In pleasure? Even she couldn't tell. Sensations swarmed through her like thousands of swirling stars, all heat and light. Before she could draw and release a breath, she was tossed into the storm.

No. Her mind all but screamed it. No one. Never. Only he had ever caused a hunger so sharp and a need so desperate. Even as her body strained against his, she struggled to remember that it wasn't enough to want. It wasn't always enough to have.

Whipped by fury and frustration, he crushed his mouth to hers, again, and then again. If only for this moment, he would prove to her that what they had together was unique to them. She would think of no one, remember nothing. Only him.

Her response tore through him, so complete, so right. The small, helpless sound that purred up from her throat shuddered into him. Like the flames that rose beside them, what they created burned and consumed. The gentle loving that had initiated them both during the night was replaced by a wild and urgent hunger that left no room for tender words and soft caresses.

She didn't want them. This was a new, a frenetic storm of needs that demanded speed and pushed for power. *Hurry.* She tore her hands from his to drag at his shirt. *Touch me.* Twin groans tangled as flesh met flesh. *More.* With a new aggression, she rolled onto him to take her mouth on a frantic race over his body. And still it wasn't enough.

His breath ragged, he stripped the layers of clothing from her, not caring about what he tore. One driving need was prominent. To possess. Hands gripped. Fingers pressed. Mouths devoured.

Agile and electric, she moved over him. Her face glowed, fragile porcelain in the firelight. Her body arched, magnificent in its new power, sheened with passion, shuddering from it, strengthened by it.

For one glorious moment she rose, witchlike, over him, her hands lifting up into her hair, her head thrown back as she lost herself in the wonder. Her body shuddered once, twice, as separate explosions burst within her. Even as she gasped, he gripped her hips and sheathed himself inside her.

He filled her. Not just physically. Even through the wracking pleasure she understood that. He, and only he, had found the key that opened every part of her. He, and only he, had found the way inside her heart, her mind. And somehow, without trying, she had found the way into his.

She didn't want to love him. She reached for his hands and gripped them tight. She didn't want to need him. Opening her eyes, she looked down at him. His eyes were dark and direct on hers. She knew, though she didn't speak, that he understood every thought in her head. On a sigh that was as much from despair as from delight, she bent down to press her mouth to his.

He could taste both the needs and the fears. He was determined to exploit the first and drive away the second. Staying deep inside her, he pushed up so that he could wrap his arms around her. He watched her eyes widen, stunned with pleasure, glazed with passion. Her fingers dug into his back. Her cry of release was muffled against his mouth seconds before he let himself go.

Bundled in a large, frayed robe, her feet covered with thick rag socks, Cilla sampled the chili. She liked sitting in the warm golden light in the kitchen, seeing the blanket of snow outside the windows, hearing the quiet moan of the wind through the pines. What surprised her, and what she wasn't ready to consider too carefully, was this feeling of regret that the weekend was almost over.

"Well?"

At Boyd's question, she looked back from the window. He sat across from her, his hair still mussed from her hands. Like her, he wore only a robe and socks. Though it made no sense, Cilla found the meal every bit as intimate as their loving in front of the fire.

Uneasy, she broke a piece of the hot, crusty bread on her plate. She was afraid he was going to bring up marriage again.

"Well what?"

"How's the chili?"

"The— Oh." She spooned up another bite, not sure if she was relieved or disappointed. "It's great. And surprising." Nervous again, she reached for her wine. "I'd have thought someone in your position would have a cook and wouldn't know how to boil an egg."

"My position?"

"I mean, if I could afford to hire a cook I wouldn't hassle with making sandwiches."

It amused him that his money made her uncomfortable. "After we're married we can hire one if you want."

Very carefully she set down her spoon. "I'm not going to marry you."

He grinned. "Wanna bet?"

"This isn't a game."

"Sure it is. The biggest in town."

She made a low sound of frustration. Picking up her spoon again, she began to tap it against the wood. "That's such a typically male attitude. It's all a game. You Tarzan, me stupid." His laughter only enraged her further. "Why is it men think women can't resist them—for sex, for companionship, for handling the details of life? Oh, Cilla, you need me. Oh, Cilla, I just want to take care of you. I want to show you what life's all about."

He considered a moment. "I don't remember saying any of those things. I think what I said is I love you and I want to marry you."

"It's the same thing."

"Not even close." He continued to eat, undisturbed.

"Well, I don't want to marry you, but I'm sure that won't make a difference. It never does."

He shot her one brief and dangerous look. "I warned you not to compare me to him. I meant it."

"I'm not just talking about Paul. I wasn't even thinking about Paul." After pushing her bowl aside, she sprang up to find a cigarette. "I hadn't given him a thought in years before all of this." She blew out an agitated stream of smoke. "And if I want to compare you to other men, I will."

He topped off his wine, then hers. "How many others have asked you to marry them?"

"Dozens." It was an exaggeration, but she didn't give a damn. "But somehow I've found the strength to resist."

"You weren't in love with them," he pointed out calmly.

"I'm not in love with you." Her voice had a desperate edge to it, and she had the sinking feeling that they both knew she was lying.

He knew, but it still hurt. The hurt settled into a dull, grinding ache in his belly. Ignoring it, he finished off his chili. "You're crazy about me, O'Roarke. You're just too pigheaded to admit it."

"I'm pigheaded?" Stifling a scream, she crushed out the cigarette. "I'm amazed that even you have the nerve to toss that one out. You haven't listened to a simple no since the day I met you."

"You're right." His gaze skimmed down her. "And look where it's got me."

"Don't be so damn smug. I'm not going to marry you, because I don't want to get married, because you're a cop and because you're rich."

"You are going to marry me," he said, "because we both know you'd be miserable without me."

"Your arrogance is insufferable. It's just as irritating—and just as pathetic—as moon-eyed pleading."

"I'd rather be smug," he decided.

"You know, you're not the first jerk I've had to shake off." She snatched up her wine before she began to pace. "In my business, you get good at it." She whirled back, stabbing a finger at him. "You're almost as bad as this kid I had to deal with in Chicago. Up to now, he's taken the prize for arrogance. But even he didn't sit there with a stupid grin on his face. With him it was flowers and poetry. He was just as much of a mule, though. I was in love with him, too. But I wouldn't admit it. I needed him to take care of me, to protect me, to make my life complete." She spun in a quick circle. "What nerve! Before you, I thought he couldn't be topped. Hounding me at the station," she muttered. "Hounding me at the apartment. Sending me an engagement ring."

"He bought you a ring?"

She paused long enough for a warning look. "Don't get any ideas, Slick."

Boyd kept his voice very cool, very even. "You said he bought you a ring. A diamond?"

"I don't know." She dragged a hand through her hair. "I didn't have it appraised. I sent it back."

"What was his name?"

She waved a hand dismissively. "I don't know how I got off on this. The point I'm trying to make is—"

"I said, what was his name?"

He rose as he asked. Cilla took a confused step back. He wasn't just Boyd now. He was every inch a cop. "I— It was John something. McGill... No, McGillis, I think. Look, he was just a pest. I only brought it up because—"

"You didn't work with a John McGillis in Chicago."

"No." Annoyed with herself, she sat down again. "We're getting off the subject, Boyd."

"I told you to tell me about anyone you were involved with."

"I wasn't involved with him. He was just a kid. Starstruck or something. He listened to the show and got hung up. I made the mistake of being nice to him, and he misunderstood. Eventually I set him straight, and that was that."

"How long?" Boyd asked quietly. "Just how long did he bother you?"

She was feeling more foolish by the minute. She could barely remember the boy's face. "Three or four months, maybe."

"Three or four months," he repeated. Taking her by the arms, he lifted her to her feet. "He kept this up for three or four months and you didn't mention it to me?"

"I never thought of it."

He resisted the temptation to give her a good shake, barely. "I want you to tell me everything you remember about him. Everything he said, everything he did."

"I can't remember."

"You'd better." Releasing her, he stepped back. "Sit down."

She obeyed. He had shaken her more than he realized. She tried to comfort herself with the fact that they were no longer arguing about marriage. But he had reminded her of something she'd allowed herself to forget for hours.

"All right. He was a night stocker at a market, and he listened to the show. He'd call in on his break, and we'd talk a little. I'd play his requests. One day I did a remote—I can't remember where—and he showed up. He seemed like a nice kid. Twenty-three or four, I guess. Pretty," she remembered. "He had a pretty, sort of harmless face. I gave him an autograph. After that he started to write me at the station. Send poems. Just sweet, romantic stuff. Nothing suggestive."

"Go on."

"Boyd, really—"

"Go on."

The best she could do was a muttered oath. "When I realized he was getting in too deep, I pulled back. He asked me out, and I told him no." Embarrassed, she blew out a breath. "A couple of times he was waiting out in the parking lot when I got off my shift. He never touched me. I wasn't afraid of him. He was so pathetic that I felt sorry for him, and that was another mistake. He misunderstood. I guess he followed me home from work, because he started to show up at the apartment. He'd leave flowers and slip notes under the door. Kid stuff," she insisted.

"Did he ever try to get in?"

"He never tried to force his way in. I told you he was harmless."

"Tell me more."

She rubbed her hands over her face. "He'd just beg. He said he loved me, that he would always love me and we were meant to be together. And that he knew I loved him, too. It got worse. He would start crying when he called. He talked about killing himself if I didn't marry him. I got the package with the ring, and I sent it back with a letter. I was cruel. I felt I had to be. I'd already accepted the job here in Denver. It was only a few weeks after the business with the ring that we moved."

"Has he contacted you since you've been in Denver?"

"No. And it's not him who's calling. I know I'd recognize his voice. Besides, he never threatened me. Never. He was obsessed, but he wasn't violent."

"I'm going to check it out." He rose, then held out a hand. "You'd better get some sleep. We're going to head back early."

She didn't sleep. Neither did he. And they lay in the dark, in silence; there was another who kept vigil through the night.

He lit the candles. New ones he'd just bought that afternoon. Their wicks were as white as the moon. They darkened and flared as he set the match against them. He lay back on the bed with the picture pressed against his naked breast—against the twin blades of the tattooed knives.

Though the hour grew late, he remained alert. Anger fueled him. Anger and hate. Beside him the radio hummed, but it wasn't Cilla's voice he heard.

She had gone away. He knew she was with that man, and she would have given herself to that man. She'd had no right to go. She belonged to John. To John, and to him.

She was beautiful, just as John had described her. She had deceptively kind eyes. But he knew better. She was cruel. Evil. And she deserved to die. Almost lovingly, he reached down a hand to the knife that lay beside him.

He could kill her the way he'd been taught. Quick and clean. But there was little satisfaction in that, he knew. He wanted her to suffer first. He wanted her to beg. As John had begged.

When she was dead, she would be with John. His brother would rest at last. And so would he.

# Chapter 10

The heat was working overtime in the precinct, and so was Boyd. While Maintenance hammered away at the faulty furnace, he pored over his files. He'd long since forsaken his jacket. His shoulder holster was strapped over a Denver P.D. T-shirt that had seen too many washings. He'd propped open a window in the conference room so that the stiff breeze from outside fought with the heat still pouring through the vents.

Two of his ongoing cases were nearly wrapped, and he'd just gotten a break in an extortion scam he and Althea had been working on for weeks. There was a court appearance at the end of the week he had to prepare for. He had reports to file and calls to make, but his attention was focused on O'Roarke, Priscilla A.

Ignoring the sweat that dribbled down his back, he read over the file on Jim Jackson, KHIP's all-night man. It interested and annoyed him.

Cilla hadn't bothered to mention that she had worked with Jackson before, in Richmond. Or that Jackson had been fired for drinking on the job. Not only had he broadcast rambling streams of consciousness, but he had taken to nodding off at the mike and leaving his audience with that taboo of radio. Dead air.

He'd lost his wife, his home and his prime spot as the morning jock and program director on Richmond's number-two Top 40 station.

When he'd gotten the ax, Cilla had taken over his duties as program director. Within six months, the number-two station had been number one. And Jackson had been picked up for drunk and disorderly.

As Althea stepped into the conference room carrying two dripping cans of soda, Boyd tossed the Jackson file across the table. Saying nothing, she passed one can to Boyd, popped the top on the second, then glanced at the file.

"He's clean except for a couple of D and D's," Althea commented.

"Revenge is high on the list for this kind of harassment. Could be he's carrying a grudge because she replaced him in Richmond and outdid him." Boyd took a swig of the warming soda. "He's only had the night spot in Denver for three months. The station manager in Richmond claims Jackson got pretty bent when they let him go. Tossed around some threats, blamed Cilla for undermining his position. Plus, you add a serious drinking problem to the grudge."

"You want to bring him in?"

"Yeah. I want to bring him in."

"Okay. Why don't we make it a doubleheader?" She picked up the file on Nick Peters. "This guy looks harmless—but then I've dated harmless-looking guys before and barely escaped with my skin. He doesn't date at all.'' She shrugged out of her turquoise linen jacket and draped it carefully over her chair back. ''It turns out that Deborah has a couple of classes with him. Over the weekend she mentioned that he pumps her for information on Cilla all the time. Personal stuff. What kind of flowers does she like? What's her favorite color? Is she seeing anyone?''

She reached in her skirt pocket and drew out a bag of jelly beans. Carefully, and after much thought, she selected a yellow one. ''Apparently he got upset when Deborah mentioned that Cilla had been married before. Deborah didn't think much of it at the time—put it down to his being weird. But she was worried enough to mention it over the weekend. She's a nice kid,'' Althea put in. ''Real sharp. She's totally devoted to Cilla.'' Althea hesitated. ''Over the course of the weekend, she told me about their parents.''

''We've already covered that ground.''

''I know we did.'' Althea picked up a pencil, ran it through her fingers, then set it aside again. ''Deborah seems to think you're good for her sister.'' She waited until Boyd looked up. ''I just wonder if her sister's good for you.''

''I can take care of myself, partner.''

''You're too involved, Boyd.'' She lowered her voice, though it couldn't have carried over the noise outside of the closed door. ''If the captain knew you were hung up, personally, with an assignment, he'd yank you. He'd be right.''

Boyd kicked back in his chair. He studied Althea's face, a face he knew as well as his own. Resentment simmered in him, but he controlled it. "I can still do my job, Thea. If I had any doubts about that, I'd yank myself."

"Would you?"

His eyes narrowed. "Yeah, I would. My first priority is my assignment's safety. If you want to go to the captain, that's your right. But I'm going to take care of Cilla, one way or the other."

"You're the one who's going to get hurt," she murmured. "One way or the other."

"My life. My problem."

The anger she'd hoped to control bubbled to the surface. "Damn it, Boyd, I care about you. It was one thing when you were infatuated by her voice. I didn't even see it as a problem when you met her and had a few sparks flying. But now you're talking serious stuff like marriage, and I know you mean it. She's got trouble, Boyd. She *is* trouble."

"You and I are assigned to take care of the trouble she's got. As for the rest, it's my business, Thea, so save the advice."

"Fine." Irked, she flipped open another file. "Bob Williams—Wild Bob—is so clean he squeaks. I haven't turned up a single connection with Cilla other than the station. He has a good marriage, goes to church, belongs to the Jaycees and for the last two weeks has been accompanying his wife to Lamaze classes."

"Nothing's turned up on the morning guys." Boyd took another swallow of the soda and wished it was an ice-cold beer.

"KHIP's just one big happy family."

"So it seems," Boyd mumbled. "Harrison looks solid, but I'm still checking. He's the one who hired her, and he actively pursued her, offering her a hefty raise and some tidy benefits to persuade her to move to Denver and KHIP.''

Althea meticulously chose a red jelly bean. ''What about the McGillis guy?''

''I'm expecting a call from Chicago.'' He opened another file. ''There's the maintenance man. Billy Lomus. War veteran—Purple Heart and a Silver Star in Nam. Did two tours of duty before the leg mustered him out. He seems to be a loner. Never stays in one place more than a year or so. He did drop down in Chicago for a while a couple years back. No family. No close friends. Settled in Denver about four months ago. Foster homes as a kid.''

Althea didn't look up. ''Rough.''

''Yeah.'' Boyd studied her bent head. There weren't many who knew that Althea Grayson had been shuffled from foster home to foster home as a child. ''It doesn't look like we're going to have much luck inside the station.''

''No. Maybe we'll do better with McGillis.'' She looked up, face calm, voice even. Only one who knew her well would have seen that she was still angry. ''You want to start with Jackson or Peters?''

''Jackson.''

''Okay. We'll try it the easy way first. I'll call and ask him to come in.''

''Thanks. Thea,'' he added before she could rise, ''you have to be hit before you can understand. I can't turn off my feelings, and I can't turn back from what I've been trained to do.''

She only sighed. ''Just watch your step, partner.''

He intended to. And while he was watching his step, he was going to watch Cilla's. She wouldn't care for that, Boyd thought as he continued to study the files. From the moment he had told her that he loved her she'd been trying to pull back.

But she wasn't afraid of him, he mused. She was afraid of herself. The deeper her feelings for him went, the more afraid she became to acknowledge them. Odd, but he hadn't known he would need the words. Yet he did. More than anything he could remember, he needed to have her look at him and tell him that she loved him.

A smile, a touch, a moan in the night—it wasn't enough. Not with Cilla. He needed the bond, and the promise, that verbal connection. Three words, he thought. A simple phrase that came easily, often too easily—and could change the structure of people's lives.

They wouldn't come easily to Cilla. If she ever pushed them through the self-doubts, the barrier of defense, the fear of being hurt, she would mean them with all of her heart. It was all he needed, Boyd decided. And he would never let her take them back.

For now he had to put aside his own wants and needs and be a cop. To keep her safe, he had to be what she feared most. For her sake, he couldn't afford to think too deeply about where their lives would go once he closed the files.

"Boyd?" Althea poked her head back in the door. "Jackson's on his way in."

"Good. We should be able to catch Peters before he checks in at the station. I want to—" He broke off when the phone rang beside him. "Fletcher." He held up a hand to wave Althea inside. "Yeah. I appreciate you checking into it for me." He muffled the phone for a moment. "Chicago P.D. That's right," he continued into the receiver. "John McGillis." Taking up a pencil, he began making notes on a legal pad. In midstroke he stopped, fingers tightening. "When?" His oath was strong and quiet. "Any family? He leave a note? Can you fax it? Right." On the legal pad he wrote in bold letters: Suicide.

In silence, Althea lowered a hip to the table.

"Anything you can get me. You're sure he didn't have a brother? No. I appreciate it, Sergeant." He hung up and tapped the pencil against the pad. "Son of a bitch."

"We're sure it's the same McGillis?" Althea asked.

"Yeah. Cilla gave me the information she had on him, plus a physical description. It's the same guy. He cashed himself in almost five months ago." He let out a long breath. "Slit his wrists with a hunting knife."

"It fits, Boyd." Althea leaned over to check his notes. "You said McGillis was obsessing on Cilla, that he'd threatened to kill himself if she didn't respond. The guy over the phone is blaming her for the death of his brother."

"McGillis didn't have a brother. Only child, survived by his mother."

"Brother could be an emotional term. A best friend."

"Maybe." He knew it fitted. What worried him was how Cilla would react. "The Chicago police are cooperating. They're sending us what information they've got. But I think it might be worth a trip east. We might get a lead from the mother."

Althea nodded. "Are you going to tell Cilla?"

"Yeah, I'm going to tell her. We'll talk to Jackson and Peters first, see if we can make a connection to McGillis."

Across town, Cilla dashed from the shower to the phone. She wanted it to be Boyd. She wanted him to tell her that he'd found John McGillis happily stocking shelves in Chicago. With her hair dripping down her back, she snatched up the phone.

"Hello."

"Did you sleep with him? Did you let him touch you?"

Her damp hands shook as she gripped the receiver. "What do you want?"

"Did you make promises to him the way you made promises to my brother? Doe he know you're a whore and a murderer?"

"No. I'm not. I don't know why—"

"He'll have to die, too."

Her blood froze. The fear she thought she'd come to understand clawed viciously at her throat. "No! Boyd has nothing to do with this. It's—it's between you and me, just as you've said all along."

"He's involved now. He made his choice, like you made yours when you killed my brother. When I'm finished with him, I'm coming for you. Do you remember what I'm going to do to you? Do you remember?"

"You don't have to hurt Boyd. Please. Please, I'll do anything you want."

"Yes, you will." There was laughter, too, long, eerily lilting. "You'll do anything."

"Please. Don't hurt him." She continued to shout into the phone long after the connection went dead. With a sob tearing at her throat, she slammed the receiver down and raced to the bedroom to dress.

She had to talk to Boyd. To see him, face-to-face. To make certain he was unharmed. And to warn him, she thought frantically. She wouldn't, couldn't, lose someone else she loved.

With her hair still streaming wet, she dashed down the stairs and yanked open the door. She nearly ran over Nick Peters.

"Oh, God." Her hands clutched at her chest. "Nick."

"I'm sorry." With fumbling hands, he pushed up his glasses. "I didn't mean to scare you."

"I have to go." She was already digging in her purse for her keys. "He called. I have to get to Boyd. I have to warn him."

"Hold on." Nick picked up the keys, which she'd dropped on the stoop. "You're in no shape to drive."

"I've got to get to Boyd," she said desperately, gripping Nick by his coat. "He said he would kill him."

"You're all worked up about the cop." Nick's mouth thinned. "He looks like he can handle himself."

"You don't understand," she began.

"Yeah, I understand. I understand just fine. You went away with him." The note of accusation surprised her, and unnerved her enough that she glanced toward the black-and-white sitting at her curb. Then she shook herself. It was foolish, absolutely foolish, to be afraid of Nick.

"Nick, I'm sorry, but I don't have time to talk right now. Can we get into this later, at the station?"

"I quit." He bit off the words. "I quit this morning."

"Oh, but why? You're doing so well. You have a future at KHIP."

"You don't even know," he said bitterly. "And you don't care."

"But I do." When she reached out to touch his arm, he jerked back.

"You let me make a fool of myself over you."

Oh, God, not again. She shook her head. "Nick, no."

"You wouldn't even let me get close, and then he comes along and it's all over before you let it begin. Now they want me to come down to the police station. They want to question me." His lips trembled. "They think I'm the one who's been calling you."

"There has to be a mistake—"

"How could you?" he shouted. "How could you believe I'd want to hurt you?" He dropped the keys back into her hand. "I just came by to let you know I'd quit, so you don't have to worry about me bothering you again."

"Nick, please. Wait." But he was already striding off to his car. He didn't look back.

Because her knees were weak, Cilla lowered herself to the stoop. She needed a moment, she realized. A moment to steady herself before she got behind the wheel of a car.

How could she have been so stupid, so blind, that she couldn't see that Nick's pride and ego were on the line. Now she had hurt him, simply by being unaware. Somehow she had to straighten out this mess her life had become. Then she had to start making amends.

Steadier, she rose, carefully locked the door, then walked to her car.

She hated police stations—had from the first. Fingering her plastic visitor's badge, she walked down the corridor. It had been scrubbed recently, and she caught the scent of pine cleaner over the ever-present aroma of coffee.

Phones rang. An incessant, strident, whirl of sound punctuated by voices raised to a shout or lowered to a grumble. Cilla turned into a doorway, to the heart of the noise, and scanned the room.

It was different from the cramped quarters where her mother had worked. And died. There was more space, less grime, and there was the addition of several computer work stations. The clickety-clack of keyboards was an underlying rhythm.

There were men and women, jackets off, shirts limp with sweat, though it was a windy fifty-five outside.

On a nearby bench, a woman rocked a fretful baby while a cop tried to distract it by jiggling a pair of handcuffs. Across the room, a young girl, surely just a teenager, related information to a trim woman cop in jeans and a sweatshirt. Silent tears coursed down the girl's face.

And Cilla remembered.

She remembered sitting in a corner of a squad room, smaller, hotter, dingier, than the one she stood in now. She had been five or six, and the baby-sitter had canceled because she'd been suffering from stomach flu. Cilla's mother had taken her to work—something about a report that couldn't wait to be written. So Cilla had sat in a corner with a doll and a Dr. Seuss book, listening to the phones and the voices. And waiting for her mother to take her home.

There had been a water cooler, she remembered. And a ceiling fan. She had watched the bubbles glug in the water and the blades whirl sluggishly. For hours. Her mother had forgotten her. Until, suffering from the same bug as her sitter, Cilla had lost her breakfast all over the squad room floor.

Shaky, Cilla wiped a hand over her damp brow. It was an old memory, she reminded herself. And not all of it. After she had been sick, her mother had cleaned her up, held her, taken her home and pampered her for the rest of the day. It wasn't fair to anyone to remember only the unhappy side.

But as she stood there she could feel all too clearly the dragging nausea, the cold sweat, and the misery of being alone and forgotten.

Then she saw him, stepping from another room. His T-shirt was damp down the front. Jackson was behind him, his hat in place, his face sheened with sweat and nerves. Flanking him was Althea.

Jackson saw her first. He took a hesitant step toward her, then stopped and shrugged. Cilla didn't hesitate. She walked to him to take his hand in both of hers.

"You okay?"

"Sure." Jackson shrugged again, but his fingers held tight on hers. "We just had to clear some things up. No big deal."

"I'm sorry. Look, if you need to talk, you can wait for me."

"No, I'm okay. Really." He lifted a hand to adjust his cap. "I guess if you screw up once you've got to keep paying for it."

"Oh, Jim."

"Hey, I'm handling it." He gave her a quick smile. "I'll catch you tonight."

"Sure."

"We appreciate your cooperation, Mr. Jackson," Althea put in.

"I told you, anything I can do to help Cilla, I'll do. I owe you," he said to Cilla, cutting her off before she could shake her head. "I owe you," he repeated, then crossed the room into the corridor.

"I could have told you that you were wasting your time with him," Cilla stated.

Boyd only nodded. "You could have told us a lot of things."

"Maybe." She turned back to him. "I need to talk to you, both of you."

"All right." Boyd gestured toward the conference room. "It's a little quieter in here."

"You want something cold?" Althea began before they settled. "I think they've finally fixed the furnace, but it's still like an oven in here."

"No, thanks. This won't take long." She sat, Althea across from her, Boyd at the table's head. She wanted to choose her words carefully. "Can I ask why you brought Jackson in?"

"You worked together in Richmond." Boyd shoved a file aside. "He had a drinking problem that got him fired, and you took over his job. He wasn't too happy about it at the time."

"No, he wasn't."

"Why didn't you tell us about it, Cilla?"

"I didn't think of it." She lifted a hand. "I honestly didn't think of it. It was a long time ago, and Jackson's come a long way. I'm sure he told you he's been in AA for over three years. He made a point of coming to see me when I was doing my run in Chicago. He wanted me to know he didn't blame me for what had happened. He's been putting his life back together."

"You got him the job at KHIP," Boyd added.

"I put in a good word for him," she said. "I don't do the hiring. He was a friend, he needed a break. When he's sober, Jackson's one of the best. And he wouldn't hurt a fly."

"And when he's drunk he breaks up bars, threatens women and drives his car into telephone poles."

"That was a long time ago," Cilla said, struggling for calm. "And the point is, he is sober. There are some things you have to forgive and forget."

"Yes." He watched her carefully. "There are."

She thought of her mother again, and of that painful memory of the squad room. "Actually, I didn't come here to talk to you about Jackson. I got another call at home."

"We know." Althea's voice was brisk and professional. "They relayed the information to us here."

"Then you know what he said." Finding Althea's cool gaze unsympathetic, Cilla turned to Boyd. "He wants to hurt you now. He knows you're involved with me, and he's dragged you into whatever sick plans he has."

"They traced the call to another phone booth, just a couple of blocks from your house," Boyd began.

"Didn't you hear me?" Cilla slapped a fist on the table. Pencils jumped. "He's going to try to kill you, too."

He didn't reach for her hand to soothe her. At the moment, he thought, she needed him more professionally than personally. "Since I'm protecting you, he would have had to try all along. Nothing's changed."

"Everything's changed," she burst out. "It doesn't matter to him if you're with the police or not, it only matters that you're with me. I want you off the case. I want you reassigned. I don't want you anywhere near me until this is over."

Boyd crushed a disposable cup in his hand and tossed it in a wastebasket. "Don't be ridiculous."

"I'm not being ridiculous. I'm being practical." She turned to Althea, her eyes full of pleas. "Talk to him. He'll listen to you."

"I'm sorry," she said after a moment. "I agree with him. We both have a job to do, and at the moment you're it."

Desperate, Cilla whipped back to Boyd. "I'll go to your captain myself."

"He already knows about the call."

She sprang up. "I'll tell him I'm sleeping with you."

"Sit down, Cilla."

"I'll insist he take you off the case."

"Sit down," Boyd repeated. His voice was still mild, but this time she relented and dropped back in her chair. "You can go to the captain and request another officer. You can demand one. It won't make any difference. If he takes me off the case, I'll just turn in my badge."

Her head snapped up at that. "I don't believe you."

"Try me."

He was too calm, Cilla realized. And too determined. Like a brick wall, she thought in despair. Going head-to-head with him when he was like this was futile. "Boyd, don't you realize I couldn't handle it if anything happened to you?"

"Yes," he said slowly. "I think I do. Then you should realize I'm just as vulnerable where you're concerned."

"That's the whole point." She broke down enough to take his hands. "You are vulnerable. Listen to me." Desperate, she pulled his hand to her cheek. "For eight years I've wondered if it had been anyone else in the room with my mother that day, anyone else but my father, would she have been sharper, would she have been quicker. Would her concentration have been more focused. Don't make me have to ask that same question about you for the rest of my life."

"Your mother wasn't prepared. I am."

"Nothing I say is going to change your mind."

"No. I love you, Cilla. One day soon you're going to have to learn to accept that. In the meantime, you're going to have to trust me."

She took her hand away to drop it into her lap. "Then there's nothing more to say."

"There's this." He pulled a file closer. She was already upset, he mused. Already on edge. But they couldn't afford to wait. "John McGillis."

Her head aching, Cilla pressed the heels of her hands to her eyes. "What about him?"

"He's dead."

Slowly she lowered her hands. "Dead?" she repeated dully. "But he was just a kid. Are you sure? Are you sure it's the same one?"

"Yes." The man wished he could spare her this. The cop knew he couldn't. "He committed suicide about five months ago."

For a moment she only stared. The blood drained out of her face, inch by inch, until it was bone white. "Oh, God. Oh, dear God. He— He threatened, but I didn't believe—"

"He was unstable, Cilla. He'd been in and out of therapy since he was fourteen. Trouble with his mother, in school, with his contemporaries. He'd already attempted suicide twice before."

"But he was so quiet. He tried so hard to make me—" She stopped, squeezing her eyes shut. "He killed himself after I left Chicago to come here. Just as he said he would."

"He was disturbed," Althea said gently. "Deeply disturbed. A year before he contacted you he was involved with a girl. When she broke things off, he swallowed a fistful of barbiturates. He was in a clinic for a while. He'd only been out for a few weeks when he made the connection with you."

"I was cruel to him." Cilla turned her purse over and over on her lap. "Really cruel. At the time I thought it was the best way to handle it. I thought he would be hurt, maybe hate me for a little while, then find some nice girl and . . . But he won't."

"I'm not going to tell you it wasn't your fault, because you're smart enough to know that yourself." Boyd's voice was deliberately devoid of sympathy.

"What McGillis did he did to himself. You were just an excuse."

She gave a quick, involuntary shudder. "It's not as easy for me. I don't live with death the way you do."

"It's never easy, not for anyone." He opened the file. "But there are priorities here, and mine is to make the connection between McGillis and the man we're after."

"You really think John's the reason I'm being threatened?"

"It's the only thing that fits. Now I want you to tell us everything you remember about him."

She released her death grip on the bag, then carefully folded her hands on the table. As clearly as possible, she repeated everything she'd already told him.

"Did you ever see him with anyone?" Boyd asked. "Did he ever talk about his friends, his family?"

"He was always alone. Like I told you, he used to call the station. I didn't meet him face-to-face for weeks. After I did, all he really talked about was the way he felt about me. The way he wanted us to be together." Her fingers twisted together. "He used to send me notes, and flowers. Little presents. It isn't that unusual for a fan to develop a kind of fantasy relationship with a jock. But then I began to see that it wasn't—" she cleared her throat "—it wasn't the normal kind of weird, if you know what I mean."

Boyd nodded and continued to write on the pad. "Go on."

"The notes became more personal. Not sexual so much as emotional. The only time he got out of hand was when he showed me his tattoo. He had these knives tattooed on his chest. It seemed so out of character for

him, and I told him I thought it was foolish for him to
mark up his body that way. We were out in the parking
lot. I was tired and annoyed, and here was this kid
pulling open his shirt to show me this stupid tattoo. He
was upset that I didn't like it. Angry, really. It was the
only time I saw him angry. He said that if it was good
enough for his brother it was good enough for him.''

"His brother?" Boyd repeated.

"That's right."

"He didn't have a brother."

She stopped twisting her fingers. "Yes, he did. He
mentioned him a couple of times."

"By name?"

"No." She hesitated, tried to think. "No," she repeated, more certain now. "He just mentioned that his
brother was living out in California. He hadn't seen him
for a couple of months. He wanted me to meet him.
Stuff like that."

"He didn't have a brother." Althea turned the file
around to skim the top sheet again. "He was an only
child."

Cilla shook her head. "So he made it up."

"No." Boyd sat back, studying his partner and Cilla
in turn. "I don't think the man we're after is a figment
of John McGillis's imagination."

# Chapter 11

Her head was pounding in a dull, steady rhythm that made her ears ring. It was too much to absorb all at once. The phone call, Nick's visit, the reminders at the station house. John McGillis's suicide.

For the first time in her life, Cilla was tempted to shut herself in her room, lock the door and escape into a drugged sleep. She wanted peace, a few hours of peace, without guilt, without dreams, without fears.

No, she realized. More than that, much more than that, she wanted control over her life again. She'd taken that control for granted once, but she would never do so again.

She could think of nothing to say to Boyd as he followed her into the house. She was much too tired to argue, particularly since she knew the argument would be futile on her side. He wouldn't take himself off the case. He wouldn't believe her when she told him they could have no future. He refused to understand that in both instances she was looking out for his best interests.

Going to the kitchen, she went directly to the cupboard above the sink. From a bottle she shook out three extra-strength aspirin.

Boyd watched her fill a glass from the tap and swallow the pills. Her movements were automatic and just a little jerky. As she rinsed the glass, she stared out the window at the backyard.

There were daffodils, their yellow blooms still secreted in the protective green. Along the low fence they sprang up like slender spears, promising spring. She hadn't known they were there when she'd bought the house.

She wished they were blooming now so that she could see those cheerful yellow trumpets waving in the breeze. How bad could life be if you could look through your own window and see flowers blooming?

"Have you eaten?" he asked her.

"I don't remember." She folded her arms and looked out at the trees. There was the faintest hint of green along the branches. You had to look hard to see it. She wondered how long it would take for the leaves to unfurl and make shade. "But I'm not hungry. There's probably something around if you are."

"How about a nap?" He brought his hands to her shoulders and massaged them gently.

"I couldn't sleep yet." On a quiet sigh, she lifted a hand up to lay it over his. "In a few weeks I'll have to cut the grass. I think I'll like that. I've never had a lawn to mow before."

"Can I come over and watch?"

She smiled, as he'd wanted her to. "I love it here," she murmured. "Not just the house, though it means a lot to stand here, just here, and look out at something that belongs to me. It's this place. I haven't really felt at home anywhere since I left Georgia. It wasn't even something I realized until I came here and felt at home again."

"Sometimes you find what you want without looking."

He was talking of love, she knew. But she was afraid to speak of it.

"Some days the sky is so blue that it hurts your eyes. If you're downtown on one of those days when the wind has swept through and cleared everything, the buildings look painted against the sky. And you can see the mountains. You can stand on the corner in the middle of rush hour and see the mountains. I want to belong here."

He turned her to him. "You do."

"I never really believed that things could last. But I was beginning to, before this. I'm not sure I can belong here, or anywhere, until I can stop being afraid. Boyd." She lifted her hands to his face. Intense, she studied him, as if to memorize every plane, every angle. "I'm not just talking about belonging to a place, but to a person. I care for you more than I've cared for anyone in my life but Deborah. And I know that's not enough."

"You're wrong." He touched his lips to hers. "It's exactly enough."

She gave him a quick, frustrated shake of her head. "You just won't listen."

"Wrong again. I listen, Cilla. I just don't always agree with what you say."

"You don't have to agree, you just have to accept."

"Tell you what—when this is over, you and I will have a nice, long talk about what we both have to accept."

"When this is over, you might be dead." On impulse, she gripped him harder. "Do you really want to marry me?"

"You know I do."

"If I said I'd marry you, would you take yourself off the case? Would you let someone else take over and go up to your cabin until it's done?"

He struggled against a bitter anger. "You should know better than to try to bribe a public servant."

"I'm not joking."

"No." His eyes hardened. "I wish you were."

"I'll marry you, and I'll do my best to make you happy if you do this one thing for me."

He set her aside and stepped back. "No deal, O'Roarke."

"Damn it, Boyd."

He jammed his hands into his pockets before he exploded. "Do you think this is some kind of trade-off? What you want for what I want? Damn you, we're talking about marriage. It's an emotional commitment and a legal contract, not a bartering tool. What's next?" he demanded. "I give up my job and you agree to have my child?"

Shock and shame robbed her of speech. She held up both hands, palms out. "I'm sorry. I'm sorry," she managed. "I didn't mean for it to sound like that. I just keep thinking of what he said today. How he said it. And I can imagine what it would be like if you weren't here." She shut her eyes. "It would be worse than dying."

"I am here." He reached for her again. "And I'm going to stay here. Nothing's going to happen to either of us."

She pulled him close, pressed her face to his throat. "Don't be angry. I just haven't got a good fight in me right now."

He relented and lifted a hand to her hair. "We'll save it for later, then."

She didn't want to think about later. Only now. "Come upstairs," she whispered. "Make love with me."

Hand in hand they walked through the empty house, up the stairs. In the bedroom she closed the door, then locked it. The gesture was a symbol of her need to lock out everything but him for this one moment in time.

The sun came strong through the windows, but she felt no need for dim lights or shadows. There would be no secrets between them here. With her eyes on his, she began to unbutton her shirt.

Only days before, she thought, she would have been afraid of this. Afraid she would make the wrong move, say the wrong word, offer too much, or not enough. He had already shown her that she had only to hold out a hand and be willing to share.

They undressed in silence, not yet touching. Did he sense her mood? she wondered. Or did she sense his? All she knew was that she wanted to look, to absorb the sight of him.

There was the way the light streamed through the window and over his hair—the way his eyes darkened as they skimmed over her. She wanted to savor the line of his body, the ridges of muscle, the smooth, taut skin.

Could she have any idea how exciting she was? he wondered. Standing in the center of the room, her clothes pooled at her feet, her skin already flushed with anticipation, her eyes clouded and aware?

He waited. Though he wanted to touch her so badly his fingers felt singed, he waited.

She came to him, her arms lifted, her lips parted. Slim, soft, seductive, she pressed against him. Still, he waited. His name was a quiet sigh as she brought her mouth to his.

Home. The thought stirred inside her, a trembling wish. He was home to her. The strength of his arms, the tenderness of his hands, the unstinting generosity of his heart. Tears burned the backs of her lids as she lost herself in the kiss.

He felt the change, the slow and subtle yielding. It aroused unbearably. Strong, she was like a flame, smoldering and snapping with life and passion. In surrender, she was like a drug that seeped silently into his blood.

Lured by, lost in, her total submission, he lowered her to the bed. Her body was his. And so for the first time, he felt, was her mind, and her heart. He was careful to treat each gently.

So sweet, she thought dreamily. So lovely. The patient stroke of his fingers, the featherbrush of his lips, turned the bright afternoon into the rich secrets of midnight. Now that she knew where he could take her, she craved the journey all the more.

No dark thoughts. No nagging fears. Like flowers on the verge of blooming, she wanted to celebrate life, the simplicity of being alive and capable of love.

He aroused her thoroughly, thoughtfully, torturously. Her answering touch and her answering kiss were just as generous. What she murmured to him were not demands, but promises she desperately wanted to keep.

They knelt together in the center of the bed, lips curved as they touched, bodies almost painfully in tune. Her hair flowed through his fingers. His skin quivered at her light caress.

Soft, quiet sighs.

Heart-to-heart, they lowered again. Mouth teased mouth. Their eyes were open when he slid into her. Joined, they held close, absorbing a fresh riot of sensation. When they moved, they moved together, with equal wonder.

The booth seemed like another world. Cilla sat at the console, studying the controls she knew so well. Both her mind and body were sluggish. The clear-sighted control she had felt for a short time with Boyd that afternoon had vanished. She wanted only for the night to be over.

He had mentioned going to Chicago the next day. She intended to encourage him. If she couldn't convince him to be reassigned, at least she would have the satisfaction of knowing he would be miles away for a day or two. Away from her, and safe, she thought.

He, whoever he was, was closing in. She could feel it. When he struck, she wanted Boyd far away.

If this man was determined to punish her for what had happened to John McGillis, she would deal with it.

Boyd had been right, to a point. She didn't blame herself for John's suicide. But she did share in the responsibility. And she couldn't keep herself from grieving for a young, wasted life.

The police would protect her, she thought as she cued up the next song. And she would protect herself. The new fear, the grinding fear, came from the fact that she didn't know how to protect Boyd.

"You're asleep at the switch," Boyd commented.

She shook herself. "No, just resting between bouts." She glanced at the clock. It was nearly midnight. Nearly time for the request line.

Once again the station was locked. There was only the two of them.

"You're nearly halfway home," he pointed out. "Look, why don't you come back to my place tonight? We can listen to my Muddy Waters records."

She decided to play dumb, because she knew it amused him. "Who?"

"Come on, O'Roarke."

It helped, a great deal, to see him grin at her. It made everything seem almost normal. "Okay, I'll listen to Muddy Whatsis—"

"Waters."

"Right—if you can answer these three music trivia questions."

"Shoot."

"Hold on." She set the next record, did a quick intro. She ruffled through her papers. "Okay, you've got three-ten to come up with them. Number one, what was the first British rock group to tour the States?"

"Ah, a trick question. The Dave Clark Five. The Beatles were the second."

"Not bad for an amateur. Number two. Who was the last performer at Woodstock."

"Jimi Hendrix. You'll have to do better, O'Roarke."

"I'm just lulling you into complacency. Number three, and this is the big one, Fletcher. What year was Buddy Holly and the Crickets' hit 'That'll Be the Day' released?"

"Going back a ways, aren't you?"

"Just answer the question, Slick."

"Fifty-six."

"Is that 1956?"

"Yeah, that's 1956."

"Too bad. It was 57. You lose."

"I want to look it up."

"Go ahead. Now you'll have to come back to my place and listen to a Rolling Stones retrospective." She yawned hugely.

"If you stay awake that long." It pleased him that she had taken a moment out to play. "Want some coffee?"

She shot him a grateful look. "Only as much as I want to breathe."

"I'll get it."

The station was empty, he thought. Since Nick Peters had gotten his ego bruised and quit, there had been no one around to brew that last pot of the evening. He, too, glanced at the clock. He wanted to have it done and be back beside her before the phones started to ring.

He'd grab her a doughnut while he was at it, Boyd decided as he checked the corridor automatically. A little sugar would help her get through the night.

Before going to the lounge, he moved to the front of the building to check the doors. The locks were in place, and the alarm was engaged. His car was alone on the lot. Satisfied, he walked through the building and gave the same careful check to the rear delivery doors before he turned into the lounge.

It wasn't going to go on much longer. With the McGillis lead, Boyd had every confidence they would tie someone to the threats in a matter of days. It would be good to see Cilla without those traces of fear in her eyes, that tension in the set of her shoulders.

The restlessness would remain, he thought. And the energy. They were as much a part of her as the color of her hair.

He added an extra scoop of coffee to the pot and listened to her voice over the speaker as she segued from one record to the next.

That magic voice, he thought. He'd had no idea when he first heard it, when he was first affected by it, that he would fall in love with the woman behind it.

It was Joan Jett now, blasting out ''I Love Rock and Roll.'' Though the lounge speaker was turned down to little more than a murmur, the feeling gritted out. It should be Cilla's theme song, he mused. Though he'd learned in their two days in his cabin that she was just as easily fascinated by the likes of Patsy Cline or Ella Fitzgerald.

What they needed was a good solid week in the mountains, he decided. Without any outside tensions to interfere.

He took an appreciative sniff of the coffee as it began to brew and hoped that he could get to Chicago, find the answers he needed and make the trip back quickly.

He whirled, disturbed by some slight sound in the corridor. A rustle. A creak of a board. His hand was already on the butt of his weapon. Drawing it, turning his back to the side wall, he took three careful strides to the doorway, scanning.

Getting jumpy, he told himself when he saw nothing but the empty halls and the glare of security lights. But instinct had him keeping the gun in his hand. He'd taken the next step when the lights went out.

Cursing under his breath, he moved fast. Though he held his weapon up for safety, he was prepared to use it. Above, from the speakers, the passionate music continued to throb. Up ahead he could see the faint glow of lights from the booth. She was there, he told himself. Safe in those lights. Keeping his back to the wall, skimming his gaze up and down the darkened hallway, he moved toward her.

As he rounded the last turn in the hallway before the booth, he heard something behind him. He saw the storeroom door swing open as he whirled. But he never saw the knife.

"That was Joan Jett and the Blackhearts coming at you. It's 11:50, Denver and a balmy forty-two degrees." Cilla frowned at the clock and wondered why Boyd was taking so long. "A little reminder that you can catch KHIP's own Wild Bob tomorrow at the Brown Palace Hotel downtown on 17th. And hey, if you've never been there, it's a very classy place. Tickets are still available for the banquet benefiting abused children. So open your wallets. It's twenty dollars stag, forty if you take your sweetie. The festivities start at seven o'clock, and Wild Bob will be spinning those discs for you.'' She potted up the next song. ''Now get ready for a doubleheader to take you to midnight. This is Cilla O'Roarke. We've got the news, then the request line, coming up.''

She switched off her mike. Shrugging her shoulders to loosen them, she slipped off the headphones. She was humming to herself as she checked the program director's hot clock. A canned ad was next, then she'd *seg* into the news at the top of the hour. She pushed away from the console to set up for the next segment.

It was then that she saw that the corridor beyond the glass door was dark. At first she only stared, baffled. Then the blood rushed to her head. If the security lights were out, the alarm might be out, as well.

He was here. Sweat pearled cold on her brow as she gripped the back of her chair. There would be no call tonight, because he was here. He was coming for her.

A scream rose in her throat to drown in a flood of panic.

Boyd. He had also come for Boyd.

Propelled by a new terror, she hit the door at a run.

''Boyd!'' She shouted for him, stumbling in the dark. Her forward motion stopped when she saw the shadow move toward her. Though it was only a shape, formless in the darkened corridor, she knew. Groping behind her, she stepped back. ''Where's Boyd? What have you done with him?'' She stepped back again. The lights from the booth slanted through the glass and split the dark in two.

She started to speak again, to beg, then nearly fainted with relief. ''Oh, God, it's you. I didn't know you were here. I thought everyone had left.''

"Everyone's gone," he answered. He moved fully into the light. And smiled. Cilla's relief iced over. He held a knife, a long-bladed hunting knife already stained with blood.

"Boyd," she said again.

"He can't help you now. No one can. We're all alone. I've waited a long time for us to be alone."

"Why?" She was beyond fear now. It was Boyd's blood on the blade, and grief left no room for fear. "Why, Billy?"

"You killed my brother."

"No. No, I didn't." She stepped back, into the booth. Hot hysteria bubbled in her throat. A cold chill sheened her skin. "I didn't kill John. I hardly knew him."

"He loved you." He limped forward, the knife in front of him, his eyes on hers. His feet were bare. He wore only camouflage pants and dark stocking cap pulled low over his graying hair and brows. Though he had smeared his face and chest and arms with black, she could see the tattoo over his heart. The twin to the one she had seen over John McGillis's.

"You were going to marry him. He told me."

"He misunderstood." She let out a quick gasp as he jabbed with the knife. Her chair toppled with a crash as she fell back against the console.

"Don't lie to me, you bitch. He told me everything, how you told him you loved him and wanted him." His voice lowered, wavered, whispered, like the voice over the phone, and had her numbed heart racing. "How you seduced him. He was so young. He didn't understand about women like you. But I do. I would have protected him. I always protected him. He was good." Billy wiped his eyes with the hand holding the knife,

then drew a gun out of his pocket. "Too good for you."
He fired, ramming a bullet into the board above the
controls. Cilla pressed both hands to her mouth to hold
back a scream. "He told me how you lied, how you
cheated, how you flaunted yourself."

"I never wanted to hurt John." She had to stay calm.
Boyd wasn't dead. She wouldn't believe he was dead.
But he was hurt. Somehow she had to get help. Bracing
herself on the console, she reached slowly behind her
and opened her mike, all the while keeping her eyes on
his face. "I swear, Billy, I never wanted to hurt your
brother."

"Liar," he shouted, lifting the knife to her throat.
She arched back, struggling to control her shuddering.
"You don't care about him. You never cared. You just
used him. Women like you love to use."

"I liked him." She sucked in her breath as the knife
nicked her throat. Blood trickled warm along her skin.
"He was a nice boy. He—he loved you."

"I loved him." The knife trembled in his hand, but
he pulled it back an inch. Cilla let out a long, quiet
breath. "He was the only person I ever loved, who ever
loved me. I took care of him."

"I know." She moistened her dry lips. Surely someone would come. Someone was listening. She didn't
dare take her eyes from his to glance around to the
phone, where the lights were blinking madly.

"He was only five when they sent me to that house.
I would have hated it there, like I'd hated all the other
places they'd sent me. But John lived there. He looked
up to me. He cared. He needed me. So I stayed until I
was eighteen. It was only a year and a half, but we were
brothers."

"Yes."

"I joined the Army. When I'd have leave he'd sneak out to see me. His pig of a mother didn't want him to have anything to do with me, 'cause I'd gotten in some trouble." He fired again, randomly, and shattered the glass in the top of the door. "But I liked the army. I liked it fine, and John liked my uniform."

His eyes glazed over a moment, as he remembered. "They sent us to Nam. Messed up my leg. Messed up my life. When we came back, people wanted to hate us. But not John. He was proud of me. No one else had ever been proud of me."

"I know."

"They tried to put him away. Twice." Again he squeezed the trigger. A bullet plowed into the reel-to-reel six inches from Cilla's head. Sweaty fear dried to ice on her skin. "They didn't understand him. I went to California. I was going to find us a nice place there. I just needed to find work. John was going to write poetry. Then he met you." The glaze melted away from his eyes, burned away by hate. "He didn't want to come to California anymore. He didn't want to leave you. He wrote me letters about you, long letters. Once he called. He shouldn't have spent his money, but he called all the way to California to tell me he was getting married. You wanted to get married at Christmas, so he was going to wait. I was coming back for it, because he wanted me there."

She could only shake her head. "I never agreed to marry him. Killing me isn't going to change that," she said when he leveled the gun at her. "You're right, he didn't understand me. And I guess I didn't understand him. He was young. He imagined I was something I wasn't, Billy. I'm sorry, terribly sorry, but I didn't cause his death.''

"You killed him.'' He ran the flat of the blade down her cheek. "And you're going to pay.''

"I can't stop you. I won't even try. But please, tell me what you've done with Boyd.''

"I killed him.'' He smiled a sweet, vacant smile that made the weapons he carried incongruous.

"I don't believe you.''

"He's dead.'' Still smiling, he held the knife up to the light. "It was easy. Easier than I remembered. I was quick,'' he assured her. "I wanted him dead, but I didn't care if he suffered. Not like you. You're going to suffer. I told you, remember? I told you what I was going to do.''

"If you've killed Boyd,'' she whispered, "you've already killed me.''

"I want you to beg.'' He laid the knife against her throat again. "I want you to beg the way John begged.''

"I don't care what you do to me.'' She couldn't feel the knife against her flesh. She couldn't feel anything. From a long way off came the wail of sirens. She heard them without emotion, without hope. They were coming, but they were coming too late. She looked into Billy's eyes. She understood that kind of pain, she realized. It came when the person who meant the most was taken from you.

"I'm sorry,'' she said, prepared to die. "I didn't love him.''

On a howl of rage, he struck her a stunning blow against the temple with the knife handle. He had planned and waited for weeks. He wouldn't kill her quickly, mercifully. He wouldn't. He wanted her on her knees, crying and screaming for her life.

She landed in a heap, driven down by the explosive pain. She would have wept then, with her hands covering her face and her body limp. Not for herself, but for what she had lost.

They both turned as Boyd staggered to the doorway.

Seconds. It took only seconds. Her vision cleared, her heart almost burst. Alive. He was alive.

Her sob of relief turned to a scream of terror as she saw Billy raise the gun. Then she was on her feet, struggling with him. Records crashed to the floor and were crushed underfoot as they rammed into a shelf. His eyes burned into hers. She did beg. She pleaded even as she fought him.

Boyd dropped to his knees. The gun nearly slipped out of his slickened fingers. Through a pale red mist he could see them. He tried to shout at her, but he couldn't drag his voice through his throat. He could only pray as he struggled to maintain a grip on consciousness and the gun. He saw the knife come up, start its vicious downward sweep. He fired.

She didn't hear the crashing glass or the clamor of feet. She didn't even hear the report as the bullet struck home. But she felt the jerk of his body as the knife flew out of his hand. She lost her grip on him as he slammed back into the console.

Wild-eyed, she whirled. She saw Boyd swaying on his knees, the gun held in both hands. Behind him was Althea, her weapon still trained on the figure sprawled on the floor. On a strangled cry, Cilla rushed over as Boyd fell.

"No." She was weeping as she brushed the hair from his eyes, as she ran a hand down his side and felt the blood. "Please, no." She covered his body with hers.

"You've got to move back." Althea bit down on panic as she urged Cilla aside.

"He's bleeding."

"I know." And badly, she thought. Very badly. "There's an ambulance coming."

Cilla stripped off her shirt to make a pressure bandage. Kneeling in her chemise, she bent over Boyd. "I'm not going to let him die."

Althea's eyes met hers. "That makes two of us."

## *Chapter 12*

There had been a sea of faces. They seemed to swim inside Cilla's head as she paced the hospital waiting room. It was so quiet there, quiet enough to hear the swish of crepe-soled shoes on tile or the whoosh of the elevator doors opening, closing. Yet in her head she could still hear the chaos of sirens, voices, the crackle of static on the police cruisers that had nosed together in the station's parking lot.

The paramedics had come. Hands had pulled her away from Boyd, pulled her out of the booth and into the cool, fresh night.

Mark, she remembered. It was Mark who had held her back as she'd run the gamut from hysteria to shock. Jackson had been there, steady as a rock, pushing a cup of some hot liquid into her hand. And Nick, white-faced, mumbling assurances and apologies.

There had been strangers, dozens of them, who had heard the confrontation over their radios. They had crowded in until the uniformed police set up a barricade.

Then Deborah had been there, racing across the lot in tears, shoving aside cops, reporters, gawkers, to get to her sister. It was Deborah who had discovered that some of the blood on Cilla was her own.

Now, dully, Cilla looked down at her bandaged hand. She hadn't felt the knife slice into it during the few frantic seconds she had fought with Billy. The scratch along her throat where the blade had nicked her was more painful. Shallow wounds, she thought. They were only shallow wounds, nothing compared to the deep gash in her heart.

She could still see how Boyd had looked when they had wheeled him out to the ambulance. For one horrible moment, she'd been afraid he was dead. So white, so still.

But he was alive. Althea had told her. He'd lost a lot of blood, but he was alive.

Now he was in surgery, fighting to stay that way. And she could only wait.

Althea watched her pace. For herself, she preferred to sit, to gather her resources and hold steady. She had her own visions to contend with. The jolt when Cilla's voice had broken into the music. The race from the precinct to the radio station. The sight of her partner kneeling on the floor, struggling to hold his weapon. He had fired only an instant before her.

She'd been too late. She would have to live with that.

Now her partner, her friend, her family, was lying on an operating table. And she was helpless.

Rising, Deborah walked across the room to put an arm around her sister. Cilla stopped pacing long enough to stare out the window.

"Why don't you lie down?" Deborah suggested.

"No, I can't."

"You don't have to sleep. You could just stretch out on the couch over there."

Cilla shook her head. "So many things are going through my mind, you know? The way he'd just sit there and grin after he'd gotten me mad. How he'd settle down in the corner of the booth with a book. The calm way he'd boss me around. I spent most of my time trying to push him away, but I didn't push hard enough. And now he's—"

"You can't blame yourself for this."

"I don't know who to blame." She looked up at the clock. How could the minutes go by so slowly? "I can't really think about that now. The cause isn't nearly as important as the effect."

"He wouldn't want you to take this on, Cilla."

She nearly smiled. "I haven't made a habit of doing what he wanted. He saved my life, Deb. How can I stand it if the price of that is his?"

There seemed to be no comfort she could offer. "If you won't lie down, how about some coffee?"

"Sure. Thanks."

She crossed to a pot of stale coffee resting on a hot plate. When Althea joined her, Deborah poured a second cup.

"How's she holding up?" Althea asked.

"By a thread." Deborah rubbed her gritty eyes before she turned to Althea. "She's blaming herself." Studying Althea, she offered the coffee. "Do you blame her, too?"

She hesitated, bringing the coffee to her lips first. She'd long since stopped tasting it. She looked over to the woman still standing by the window. Cilla wore baggy jeans and Mark Harrison's tailored jacket. She wanted to blame Cilla, she realized. She wanted to blame her for involving Boyd past the point of wisdom. She wanted to blame her for being the catalyst that had set an already disturbed mind on the bloody path of revenge.

But she couldn't. Neither as a cop nor as a woman.

"No," she said with a sigh. "I don't blame her. She's only one of the victims here."

"Maybe you could tell her that." Deborah passed the second cup to Althea. "Maybe that's what she needs to hear."

It wasn't easy to approach Cilla. They hadn't spoken since they had come to the waiting room. In some strange way, Althea realized, they were rivals. They both loved the same man. In different ways, perhaps, and certainly on different levels, but the emotions were deep on both sides. It occurred to her that if there had been no emotion on Cilla's part there would have been no resentment on hers. If she had remained an assignment, and only an assignment, Althea would never have felt the need to cast blame.

It seemed Boyd had not been the only one to lose his objectivity.

She stopped beside Cilla, stared at the same view of the dark studded with city lights. "Coffee?"

"Thanks." Cilla accepted the cup but didn't drink. "They're taking a long time."

"It shouldn't be much longer."

Cilla drew in a breath and her courage. "You saw the wound. Do you think he'll make it?"

*I don't know.* She almost said it. They both knew she'd thought it. "I'm counting on it."

"You told me once he was a good man. You were right. For a long time I was afraid to see that, but you were right." She turned to face Althea directly. "I don't expect you to believe me, but I would have done anything to keep him from being hurt."

"I do believe you. And you did what you could." Before Cilla could turn away again, Althea put a hand on her arm. "Opening your mike may have saved his life. I want you to think about that. With a wound as serious as Boyd's, every second counted. With the broadcast, you gave us a fix on the situation, so there was an ambulance on the scene almost as quickly as we were. If Boyd makes it, it's partially due to your presence of mind. I want you to think about that."

"Billy only went after him because of me. I have to think about that, as well."

"You're trying to logic out an irrational situation. It won't work." The sympathy vanished from her voice. "If you want to start passing out blame, how about John McGillis? It was his fantasy that lit the fuse. How about the system that allowed someone like Billy Lomus to bounce from foster home to foster home so that he never knew what it was like to feel loved or wanted by anyone but a young, troubled boy? You could blame Mark for not checking Billy's references closely enough. Or Boyd and me for not making the connection quicker. There's plenty of blame to pass around, Cilla. We're all just going to have to live with our share."

"It doesn't really matter, does it? No matter who's at fault, it's still Boyd's life on the line."

"Detective Grayson?"

Althea snapped to attention. The doctor who entered was still in surgical greens damped down the front with sweat. She tried to judge his eyes first. They were a clear and quiet gray and told her nothing.

"I'm Grayson."

His brow lifted slightly. It wasn't often you met a police detective who looked as though she belonged on the cover of *Vogue*. "Dr. Winthrop, chief of surgery."

"You operated on Boyd, Boyd Fletcher?"

"That's right. He's your partner?"

"Yes." Without conscious thought on either side, Althea and Cilla clasped hands. "Can you tell us how he is?"

"I can tell you he's a lucky man," Winthrop said. "If the knife had gone a few inches either way, he wouldn't have had a chance. As it is, he's still critical, but the prognosis is good."

"He's alive." Cilla finally managed to force the words out.

"Yes." Winthrop turned to her. "I'm sorry, are you a relative?"

"No, I . . . No."

"Miss O'Roarke is the first person Boyd will want to see when he wakes up." Althea gave Cilla's hand a quick squeeze. "His family's been notified, but they were in Europe and won't be here for several hours yet."

"I see. He'll be done in Recovery shortly. Then we'll transfer him to ICU. O'Roarke," he said suddenly. "Of course. My son's a big fan." He lifted her bandaged hand gently. "I've already heard the story. If you were my patient, you'd be sedated and in bed."

"I'm fine."

Frowning, he studied her pupils. "To put it in unprofessional terms, not by a long shot." His gaze skimmed down the long scratch on her throat. "You've had a bad shock, Miss O'Roarke. Is there someone who can drive you home?''

''I'm not going home until I see Boyd.''

''Five minutes, once he's settled in ICU. Only five. I can guarantee he won't be awake for at least eight hours.''

''Thank you.'' If he thought she would settle for five minutes, he was very much mistaken.

''Someone will come by to let you know when you can go down.'' He walked out rubbing the small of his back and thinking about a hot meal.

''I need to call the captain.'' It infuriated Althea that she was close to tears. ''I'd appreciate it if you'd come back for me after you've seen him. I'd like a moment with him myself.''

''Yes, of course. Thea.'' Letting her emotions rule, Cilla wrapped her arms around Althea. The tears didn't seem to matter. Nor did pride. They clung together and held on to hope. They didn't speak. They didn't have to. When they separated, Althea walked away to call her captain. Cilla turned blindly to the window.

''He's going to be okay,'' Deborah murmured beside her.

''I know.'' She closed her eyes. She did know. The dull edge of fear was gone. ''I just need to see him, Deb. I need to see him for myself.''

''Have you told him you love him?''

She shook her head.

''Now might be a good time.''

''I was afraid I wouldn't get the chance, and now...I don't know.''

''Only a fool would turn her back on something so special.''

"Or a coward." Cilla pressed her fingers to her lips. "Tonight, all night, I've been half out of my mind thinking he might die. Line of duty." She turned to face her sister. "In the line of duty, Deborah. If I let myself go, if I don't turn my back, how many other times might I stand here wondering if he'll live or die?"

"Cilla—"

"Or open the door one day and have his captain standing there, waiting to tell me that he was already gone, the way Mom's captain came to the door that day."

"You can't live your life waiting for the worst, Cilla. You have to live it hoping for the best."

"I'm not sure I can." Weary, she dragged her hands through her hair. "I'm not sure of anything right now except that he's alive."

"Miss O'Roarke?" Both Cilla and Deborah turned toward the nurse. "Dr. Winthrop said to bring you to ICU."

"Thank you."

Her heart hammered in her ears as she followed the nurse toward the corridor. Her mouth was dry, and her palms were damp. She tried to ignore the machines and monitors as they passed through the double doors into Intensive Care. She wanted to concentrate on Boyd.

He was still so white. His face was as colorless as the sheet that covered him. The machines blipped and hummed. A good sound, she tried to tell herself. It meant he was alive. Only resting.

Tentatively she reached out to brush at his hair. It was so warm and soft. As was his skin when she traced the back of her knuckles over his cheek.

"It's all over now," she said quietly. "All you have to do is rest and get better." Desperate for the contact, she took his limp hand in hers, then pressed it to her lips. "I'm going to stay as close as they'll let me. I promise." It wasn't enough, not nearly enough. She brushed her lips over his hair, his cheek, his mouth. "I'll be here when you wake up."

She kept her word. Despite Deborah's arguments, she spent the rest of the night on the couch in the waiting room. Every hour they allowed her five minutes with him. Every hour she woke and took what she was given.

He didn't stir.

Dawn broke, shedding pale, rosy light through the window. The shifts changed. Cilla sipped coffee and watched the night staff leave for home. New sounds began. The clatter of the rolling tray as breakfast was served. Bright morning voices replaced the hushed tones of night. Checking her watch, she set the coffee aside and walked out to sit on a bench near the doors of ICU. It was almost time for her hourly visit.

While she waited to be cleared, a group of three hurried down the hall. The man was tall, with a shock of gray hair and a lean, almost cadaverous face. Beside him was a trim woman, her blond hair ruffled, her suit wrinkled. They were clutching hands. Walking with them was another woman. The daughter, Cilla thought with dazed weariness. She had her father's build and her mother's face.

There was panic in her eyes. Even through the fatigue Cilla saw it and recognized it. Beautiful eyes. Dark green, just like . . . Boyd's.

"Boyd Fletcher," the younger woman said to the nurse. "We're his family. They told us we could see him."

The nurse checked her list. "I'll take you. Only two at a time, please."

"You go." Boyd's sister turned to her parents. "I'll wait right here."

Cilla wanted to speak, but as the woman sat on the opposite end of the bench she could only sit, clutching her hands together.

What could she say to them? To any of them? Even as she searched for words, Boyd's sister leaned back against the wall and shut her eyes.

Ten minutes later, the Fletchers came out again. There were lines of strain around the woman's eyes, but they were dry. Her hand was still gripping her husband's.

"Natalie." She touched her daughter's shoulder. "He's awake. Groggy, but awake. He recognized us." She beamed a smile at her husband. "He wanted to know what the hell we were doing here when we were supposed to be in Paris." Her eyes filled then, and, she groped impatiently for a handkerchief. "The doctor's looking at him now, but you can see him in a few minutes."

Natalie slipped an arm around her mother's waist, then her father's. "So what were we worried about?"

"I still want to know exactly what happened." Boyd's father shot a grim look at the double doors. "Boyd's captain has some explaining to do."

"We'll get the whole story," his wife said soothingly. "Let's just take a few minutes to be grateful it wasn't worse." She dropped the handkerchief back in her purse. "When he was coming around, he asked for someone named Cilla. That's not his partner's name. I don't believe we know a Cilla."

Though her legs had turned to jelly, Cilla rose. "I'm Cilla." Three pairs of eyes fixed on her. "I'm sorry," she managed. "Boyd was . . . he was hurt because . . . he was protecting me. I'm sorry," she said again.

"Excuse me." The nurse stood by the double doors again. "Detective Fletcher insists on seeing you, Miss O'Roarke. He's becoming agitated."

"I'll go with you." Taking charge, Natalie steered Cilla through the doors.

Boyd's eyes were closed again, but he wasn't asleep. He was concentrating on reviving the strength he'd lost in arguing with the doctor. But he knew the moment she entered the room, even before she laid a tentative hand on his. He opened his eyes and looked at her.

"Hi, Slick." She made herself smile. "How's it going?"

"You're okay." He hadn't been sure. The last clear memory was of Billy holding the knife and Cilla struggling.

"I'm fine." Deliberately she put her bandaged hand behind her back. Natalie noted the gesture with a frown. "You're the one hooked up to machines." Though her voice was brisk, the hand that brushed over his cheek was infinitely tender. "I've seen you looking better, Fletcher."

He linked his fingers with hers. "I've felt better."

"You saved my life." She struggled to keep it light, keep it easy. "I guess I owe you."

"Damn right." He wanted to touch her, but his arms felt like lead. "When are you going to pay up?"

"We'll talk about it. Your sister's here." She glanced across the bed at Natalie.

Natalie leaned down and pressed a kiss to his brow. "You jerk."

"It's nice to see you, too."

"You just couldn't be a pushy, uncomplicated business shark, could you?"

"No." He smiled and nearly floated off again. "But you make a great one. Try to keep them from worrying."

She sighed a little as she thought of their parents. "You don't ask for much."

"I'm doing okay. Just keep telling them that. You met Cilla."

Natalie's gaze skimmed up, measuring. "Yes, we met. Just now."

"Make her get the hell out of here." Natalie saw the shocked hurt in Cilla's eyes, saw her fingers tighten convulsively on the bedguard.

"She doesn't have to make me go." With her last scrap of pride, she lifted her chin. "If you don't want me around, I'll—"

"Don't be stupid," Boyd said in that mild, slightly irritated voice that made her want to weep. He looked back at his sister. "She's dead on her feet. Last night was rough. She's too stubborn to admit it, but she needs to go home and get some sleep."

"Ungrateful slob," Cilla managed. "Do you think you can order me around even when you're flat on your back?"

"Yeah. Give me a kiss."

"If I didn't feel sorry for you, I'd make you beg." She leaned close to touch her lips to his. At the moment of contact she realized with a new panic that she was going to break down. "Since you want me to clear out, I will. I've got a show to prep for."

"Hey, O'Roarke."

She got enough of a grip on control to look over her shoulder. "Yes?"

"Come back soon."

"Well, well..." Natalie murmured as Cilla hurried away.

"Well, well..." her brother echoed. He simply could not keep his eyes open another moment. "She's terrific, isn't she?"

"I suppose she must be."

"As soon as I can stay awake for more than an hour at a time, I'm going to marry her."

"I see. Maybe you should wait until you can actually stand up for an hour at a time."

"I'll think about it. Nat." He found her hand again. "It is good to see you."

"You bet," she said as he fell asleep.

Cilla was almost running when she hit the double doors. She didn't pause, not even when Boyd's parents both rose from the bench. As her breath hitched and her eyes filled, she hurried down the hall and stumbled into the ladies' room.

Natalie found her there ten minutes later, curled up in a corner, sobbing wretchedly. Saying nothing, Natalie pulled out a handful of paper towels. She dampened a few, then walked over to crouch in front of Cilla.

"Here you go."

"I hate to do this," Cilla said between sobbing breaths.

"Me too." Natalie wiped her own eyes, and then, without a thought to her seven-hundred-dollar suit, sat on the floor. "The doctor said they'd probably move him to a regular room by tomorrow. They're hoping to downgrade his condition from critical to serious by this afternoon."

"That's good." Cilla covered her face with the cool, wet towel. "Don't tell him I cried."

"All right."

There was silence between them as each worked on control.

"I guess you'd like to know everything that happened," Cilla said at length.

"Yes, but it can wait. I think Boyd had a point when he told you to go home and get some sleep."

With very little effort she could have stretched out on the cool tile floor and winked out like a light. "Maybe."

"I'll give you a lift."

"No, thanks. I'll call a cab."

"I'll give you a lift," Natalie repeated, and rose.

Lowering the towel, Cilla studied her. "You're a lot like him, aren't you?"

"So they say." Natalie offered a hand to help Cilla to her feet. "Boyd told me you're getting married."

"So he says."

For the first time in hours, Natalie laughed. "We really will have to talk."

She all but lived in the hospital for the next week. Boyd was rarely alone. Though it might have frustrated him from time to time that he barely had a moment for a private word with her, Cilla was grateful.

His room was always filled with friends, with family, with associates. As the days passed and his condition improved, she cut her visits shorter and kept them farther apart.

They both needed the distance. That was how she rationalized it. They both needed time for clear thinking. If she was to put the past—both the distant past and the near past—behind her, she needed to do it on her own.

It was Thea who filled her in on Billy Lomus. In his troubled childhood, the only bright spot had been John

McGillis. As fate would have it, they had fed on each
other's weaknesses. John's first suicide attempt had
occurred two months after Billy left for Viet Nam. He'd
been barely ten years old.

When Billy had returned, bitter and wounded, John
had run away to join him. Though the authorities had
separated them, they had always managed to find each
other again. John's death had driven Billy over the fine
line of reason he had walked.

"Delayed stress syndrome," Althea said as they stood
together in the hospital parking lot. "Paranoid psy-
chosis. Obsessive love. It doesn't really matter what la-
bel you put on it."

"Over these past couple of weeks, I've asked myself
dozens of times if there was anything I could have done
differently with John McGillis." She took in a deep
breath of the early spring air. "And there wasn't. I can't
tell you what a relief it is to finally be sure of that."

"Then you can put it behind you."

"Yes. It's not something I can forget, but I can put
it behind me. Before I do, I'd like to thank you for
everything you did, and tried to do."

"It was my job," Althea said simply. "We weren't
friends then. I think maybe we nearly are now."

Cilla laughed. "Nearly."

"So, as someone who's nearly your friend, there's
something I'd like to say."

"Okay."

"I've been watching you and Boyd since the beginning. Observation's also part of the job." Her eyes,
clear and blue and direct, met Cilla's. "I still haven't
decided if I think you're good for Boyd. It's not really
my call, but I like to form an opinion."

Cilla looked out beyond the parking lot to a patch of green. The daffodils were blooming there, beautifully. "Thea, you're not telling me anything I don't already know."

"My point is, Boyd thinks you're good for him. That's enough for me. I guess the only thing you've got to decide now is if he's good for you."

"He thinks he is," she murmured.

"I've noticed." In an abrupt change of mood, Althea looked toward the hospital. "I heard he was getting out in a couple of days."

"That's the rumor."

"You've already been up, I take it."

"For a few minutes. His sister's there, and a couple of cops. They brought in a flower arrangement shaped like a horseshoe. The card read Tough break, Lucky. They tried to tell him they'd confiscated it from some gangster's funeral."

"Wouldn't surprise me. Funny thing about cops. They usually have a sense of humor, just like real people." She gave Cilla an easy smile. "I'm going to go up. Should I tell him I ran into you and you're coming back later?"

"No. Not this time. Just—just tell him to listen to the radio. I'll see if I can dig up 'Dueling Banjos.' "

" 'Dueling Banjos'?"

"Yeah. I'll see you later, Thea."

"Sure." Althea watched Cilla walk to her car and was grateful, not for the first time, not to be in love.


Though the first couple of nights in the booth after the shooting had been difficult, Cilla had picked up her old routine. She no longer got a flash of Boyd bleeding as he knelt by the door, or of Billy, his eyes wild, holding a knife to her throat.

She'd come to enjoy the request line again. The blinking lights no longer grated on her nerves. Every hour she was grateful that Boyd was recovering, and so she threw herself into her work with an enthusiasm she had lost for too long.

"Cilla."

She didn't jolt at the sound of her name, but swiveled easily in her chair and smiled at Nick. "Hey."

"I, ah, decided to come back."

She kept smiling as she accepted the cup of coffee he offered. "I heard."

"Mark was real good about it."

"You're an asset to the station, Nick. I'm glad you changed your mind."

"Yeah, well..." He let his words trail off as he studied the scar on the palm of her hand. The stitches had come out only days earlier. "I'm glad you're okay."

"Me too. You want to get me the Rocco's Pizza commercial?"

He nearly jumped for it, sliding it out of place and handing it to her. Cilla popped the tape in, then potted it up.

"I wanted to apologize," he blurted out.

"You don't have to."

"I feel like a jerk, especially after I heard...well, the whole story about Billy and that guy from Chicago."

"You're nothing like John, Nick. And I'm flattered that you were attracted to me—especially since you have a class with my incredibly beautiful sister."

"Deborah's nice. But she's too smart."

Cilla had her first big laugh of the month. "Thanks a lot, kid. Just what does that make me?"

"I didn't mean—" He broke off, mortally embarrassed. "I only meant—"

"Don't bury yourself." Giving him a quick grin, she turned on her mike. "Hey, Denver, we're going to keep it rocking for you for the next quarter hour. It's 10:45 on this Thursday night, and I'm just getting started." She hit them with a blast of "Guns 'n' Roses". "Now that's rock and roll," she said to herself. "Hey, Nick, why don't you..." Her words trailed off when she saw Boyd's mother in the doorway. "Mrs. Fletcher." She sprang up, nearly strangling herself with her headphones.

"I hope I'm not disturbing you." She smiled at Cilla, nodded to Nick.

"No, no, of course not." Cilla brushed uselessly at her grimy jeans. "Um... Nick, why don't you get Mrs. Fletcher a cup of coffee?"

"No, thank you, dear. I can only stay a moment."

Nick made his excuses and left them alone.

"So," Mrs. Fletcher said after a quick study. She blinked at the posters on the wall and examined the equipment. "This is where you work?"

"Yes. I'd, ah... give you a tour, but I've got—"

"That's perfectly all right." The lines of strain were no longer around her eyes. She was a trim, attractive and perfectly groomed woman. And she intimidated the hell out of Cilla. "Don't let me interrupt you."

"No, I... I'm used to working with people around."

"I missed you at the hospital the past few days, so I thought I'd come by here and say goodbye."

"You're leaving?"

"Since Boyd is on the mend, we're going back to Paris. It's business, as well as pleasure."

Cilla made a noncommittal noise and cued up the next record. "I know you must be relieved that Boyd...well, that he's all right. I'm sure it was dreadful for you."

"For all of us. Boyd explained it all to us. You've had a horrible ordeal."

"It's over now."

"Yes." She lifted Cilla's hand and glanced at the healing wound. "Experiences leave scars. Some deeper than others." She released Cilla's hand to wander around the tiny booth. "Boyd tells me you're to be married."

"I..." She shook off the shock, cleared her throat. "Excuse me a minute." Turning to the console she segued into the next record, then pushed another switch. "It's time for our mystery record," she explained. "The roll of thunder plays over the song, then people call in. The first caller who can give me the name of the song, the artist and the year of the recording wins a pair of concert tickets. We've got Madonna coming in at the end of the month."

"Fascinating," Mrs. Fletcher smiled, a smile precisely like Boyd's. "As I was saying, Boyd tells me you're to be married. I wondered if you'd like any help with the arrangements."

"No. That is, I haven't said... Excuse me." She pounced on a blinking light. "KHIP. No, I'm sorry, wrong answer. Try again." She struggled to keep her mind clear as the calls came through. The fourth caller's voice was very familiar.

"Hey, O'Roarke."

"Boyd." She sent his mother a helpless look. "I'm working."

"I'm calling. You got a winner yet?"

"No, but—"

"You've got one now. 'Electric Avenue,' Eddy Grant, 1983."

She had to smile. "You're pretty sharp, Slick. Looks like you've got yourself a couple of concert tickets. Hold on." She switched on her mike. "We've got a winner."

Patient, Mrs. Fletcher watched her work, smiling as she heard her son's voice over the speakers.

"Congratulations," Cilla said after she'd potted up a new record.

"So, are you going to the concert with me?"

"If you're lucky. Gotta go."

"Hey!" He shouted before she could cut him off. "I haven't heard 'Dueling Banjos' yet."

"Keep listening." After a long breath, she turned back to his mother. "I'm very sorry."

"No problem, no problem at all." In fact, she'd found the interlude delightful. "About the wedding?"

"I don't know that there's going to be a wedding. I mean, there isn't a wedding." She dragged a hand through her hair. "I don't think."

"Ah, well..." That same faint, knowing smile hovered around her mouth. "I'm sure you or Boyd will let us know. He's very much in love with you. You know that?"

"Yes. At least I think I do."

"He told me about your parents. I hope you don't mind."

"No." She sat again. "Mrs. Fletcher—"

"Liz is fine."

"Liz. I hope you don't think I'm playing some sort of game with Boyd. I wouldn't ask him to change. I could never ask him to change, and I just don't know if I can live with what he does.''

"Because you're afraid of his being a policeman? Afraid he might die and leave you, as your parents did?''

Cilla looked down at her hands, spread her fingers. "I guess when you trim away all the fat, that's it.''

"I understand. I worry about him,'' she said quietly. "I also understand he's doing what he has to do.''

"Yes, it is what he has to do. I've given that a lot of thought since he was hurt.'' Cilla looked up again, her eyes intense. "How do you live with it?''

Liz took Cilla's restless hand in hers. "I love him.''

"And that's enough?''

"It has to be. It's always difficult to lose someone you love. The way you lost your parents was tragic—and, according to Boyd, unnecessary. My mother died when I was only six. I loved her very much, though I had little time with her.''

"I'm sorry.''

"She cut herself in the garden one day. Just a little nick on the thumb she paid no attention to. A few weeks later she was dead of blood poisoning. All from a little cut on the thumb with a pair of rusty garden shears. Tragic, and unnecessary. It's hard to say how and when a loved one will be taken from us. How sad it would be not to allow ourselves to love because we were afraid to lose.'' She touched a hand to Cilla's cheek. "I hope to see you again soon.''

"Mrs. Fletcher—Liz,'' Cilla said as she stopped at the door. "Thank you for coming.''

"It was my pleasure." She glanced at a poster of a bare-chested rock star with shoulder-length hair and a smoldering sneer. "Though I do prefer Cole Porter."

Cilla found herself smiling as she slipped in another tape. After the ad, she gave her listeners fifteen uninterrupted minutes of music and herself time to think.

When the request line rolled around, she was as nervous as a cat, but her mind was made up.

"This is Cilla O'Roarke for KHIP. It's five minutes past midnight and our request lines are open. Before I take a call, I've got a request of my own. This one goes to Boyd. No, it's not 'Dueling Banjos,' Slick. You're just going to have to try a new memory on for size. It's an old one by the Platters. 'Only You.' I hope you're listening, because I want you to know—" For the first time in her career, she choked on the air. "Oh, boy, it's a lot to get out. I guess I want to say I finally figured out it's only you for me. I love you, and if the offer's still open, you've got a deal."

She sent the record out and, with her eyes closed, let the song flow through her head.

Struggling for composure, she took call after call. There were jokes and questions about Boyd, but none of the callers *was* Boyd. She'd been so certain he would phone.

Maybe he hadn't even been listening. The thought of that had her dropping her head in her hands. She had finally dragged out the courage to tell him how she felt, and he hadn't been listening.

She got through the next two hours step-by-step. It had been a stupid move, she told herself. It was unbelievably foolish to announce that you loved someone over the radio. She'd only succeeded in embarrassing herself.

The more she thought about it, the angrier she became. She'd told him to listen, damn it. Couldn't he do anything she asked him to do? She'd told him to go away, he'd stayed. She'd told him she wasn't going to marry him, he'd told everyone she was. She'd told him to listen to the radio, he'd shut it off. She'd bared her soul over the public airwaves for nothing.

"That was a hell of a request," Jackson commented when he strolled into the booth just before two.

"Shut up."

"Right." He hummed to himself as he checked the programmer's clock for his shift. "Ratings should shoot right through the roof."

"If I wanted someone to be cheerful in here, I'd have brought along Mickey Mouse."

"Sorry." Undaunted, he continued to hum.

With her teeth on edge, Cilla opened her mike. "That's all for tonight, Denver. It's 1:58. I'm turning you over to my man Jackson. He'll be with you until six in the a.m. Have a good one. And remember, when you dream of me, dream good." She kicked her chair out of the way. "And if you're smart," she said to Jackson, "you won't say a word."

"Lips are sealed."

She stalked out, snatching up her jacket and digging for her keys as she headed for the door. She was going to go home and soak her head. And if Deborah had been listening and was waiting up, it would just give her someone to chew out.

Head down, hands in her pockets, she stomped to her car. She had her hand on the doorhandle before she saw that Boyd was sitting on the hood.

"Nice night," he said.

"What—what the hell are you doing here?" Anger forgotten, she rushed around the car. "You're supposed to be in the hospital. They haven't released you yet."

"I went over the wall. Come here."

"You jerk. Sitting out here in the night air. You were nearly dead two weeks ago, and—"

"I've never felt better in my life." He grabbed her by the front of her jacket and hauled her against him for a kiss. "And neither have you."

"What?"

"You've never felt better in my life, either."

She shook her head to clear it and stepped back. "Get in the car. I'm taking you back to the hospital."

"Like hell." Laughing, he pulled her against him again and devoured her mouth.

She went weak and hot and dizzy. On a little sigh, she clung to him, letting her hands rush over his face, into his hair. Just to touch him, to touch him and know he was whole and safe and hers.

"Lord, do you know how long it's been since you've kissed me like that?" He held her close, waiting for his heart rate to level. His side was throbbing in time with it. "Those chaste little pecks in the hospital weren't enough."

"We were never alone."

"You never stayed around long enough." He pressed his lips to the top of her head. "I liked the song."

"What song? Oh." She stepped back again. "You were listening."

"I liked the song a lot." He took her hand and pressed his mouth to the scar. "But I liked what you said before it even better. How about saying it again, face-to-face?"

"I . . ." She let out a huff of breath.

Patient, he cupped her face in his hands. "Come on, O'Roarke." He smiled. "Spit it out."

"I love you." She said it so quickly, and with such obvious relief, that he laughed again. "Damn it, it's not funny. I really love you, and it's your fault for making it impossible for me to do anything else."

"Remind me to pat myself on the back later. You've got a hell of a voice, Cilla." He wrapped his arms around her, comfortably. "And you've never sounded better than tonight."

"I was scared."

"I know."

"I guess I'm not anymore." She rested her head against his shoulder. "It feels right."

"Yeah. Just right. The offer still holds, Cilla. Marry me."

She took her time, not because she was afraid, but because she wanted to savor it. She wanted to remember every second. The moon was full, the stars were out. She could just catch the faintest drift of those fragile spring flowers.

"There's one question I have to ask you first."

"Okay."

"Can we really hire a cook?"

He laughed and lowered his mouth to hers. "Absolutely."

"Then it's a deal."

\* \* \* \* \*

*If you're wondering about Cilla's sister*
*Don't miss*
*NIGHT SHADOW*
*Silhouette Intimate Moments #373*
*An . . . unusual story*
*Coming in March*

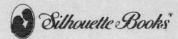

# SILHOUETTE·INTIMATE·MOMENTS®

## NORA ROBERTS
## Night Shadow

People all over the city of Urbana were asking, Who was that masked man?

Assistant district attorney Deborah O'Roarke was the first to learn his secret identity . . . and her life would never be the same.

The stories of the lives and loves of the O'Roarke sisters began in January 1991 with NIGHT SHIFT, Silhouette Intimate Moments #365. And if you want to know more about Deborah and the man behind the mask, look for NIGHT SHADOW, Silhouette Intimate Moments #373, available in March at your favorite retail outlet.

NITE-1

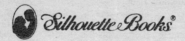

*Silhouette Books*®